ORIGEN

Beginning

Croney

1

1. Amore

Sunday, November 5, 2017, and my 35th birthday. I was on my way to see the new Thor movie, Ragnarök. I stepped out the house, locked the door and headed for my car. As I stepped off the sidewalk and unlocking the car door (beep), my peripheral noticed the full and beautiful moon. Thinking nothing else of it, I opened the car door, sat down, adjusted my rearview mirror, closed my door. As I attempted to focus, my eyes could not help but wander ever so slowly. My eyeballs went from left to right, left to right, left to right. Very confused and lowly I said, "am I in a cave?" As this information made its way through my highly confused mind, a tingling sensation crawled over my body. My heart began to pump and beat harder as the seconds raced away from me. I tried to grasp what was taking place, but so many thoughts and feelings clouded my mind. Then, a voice from within this cave echoed... "Breathe", so naturally, I freaked out! Fear ran straight through my spine, and into my bubbling guts. My teeth clenched and chattered with such intensity, I thought they were gonna chip. I began to feel myself really losing it. I started calling, "Jehovah! Jehovah, please!" I desperately called out to him. But after a few minutes, there was just me... in a cave... yelling. Starting to lose faith, I began to ask Jehovah to pardon me for all of my sins. "You know God, me and you have always seen eye to eye,

I've tried my best to live a straightforward life, except back in '99-02, sorry. But… if you could help a sister out…that would be amazing." I waited a while longer, but nothing. I began to grow anxious and when that happens, the following emotion is typically anger. But before losing my complete cool, just in case Jehovah was testing me… I counted to 100… "98 (exhale deeply), 99 (exhale even deeper), 100 damn it!... This can't possibly be the end. I haven't even met Nas yet." I closed my eyes and took four big full breaths and on that final exhale, I had enough juice to open one eye. A few minutes later, I had calmed down enough to open the other eye… (exhale) "listen up cave! I am a mother, a sister, a friend, a child of the Most High and a motherfucking G! I need you to send me back to my car… please." Then this light from the right side of the cave caught my attention. As I focused on it and as its glare settled, I noticed that there was a man sitting on the ground and it was him that was glowing. So, I shut my eyes and pinched myself "Fuck! I can feel that… Ok…Ok, so… I'm not dreaming!" So, allow me to repeat, just in case you, who's reading this is lost. **On Sunday, November 5, 2017**, I was on my way to see the new Thor movie, you know…Ragnarök. I entered my car… which put me in a cave, where there was a lit and glowing man! And as previously stated, as the moments got away from me…I was dying little by little. Ok, now back to me. I opened both eyes and stared at the glowing man. And without breaking his train of thought, he

3

raised his hand and signaled that I join him. My whole body shook in the inside, I couldn't even move if I had to save my own life! So much for me being a G, right. I didn't know what to do. I didn't even know if I should move! I didn't know what to think, I was just hoping this man was not a god damn vampire! I looked over at the man again because I could not help it. Keep in mind... he was sitting on the ground... in criss cross applesauce, while shining! This was way too much for me to process. As the moments passed, there was something about his glow. It was alluring, warm; even enchanting. You know the expression "like a moth to a flame." The glow was interesting and pleasantly enticing. It even had a sound to it...it sounded like long chanting but chopped and screwed. The longer I stared, the deeper the glow engaged me. Not sure how much time passed, but I was officially calmed down. My mood had changed completely. My body began moving forward, towards the glowing man. The glow had me under some sort of relaxation trance. I continued to move forward as my body somehow managed to now be in proximity to the man. Now I too, was sitting in criss cross applesauce facing him. As I sat there, this shiny-ness, this light started to slowly surround me. As the light got closer to me the man said "breathe". Sidebar: "I didn't trip! I low key wanted too though!"

I took the man's advice without so much as thinking about it. As the breaths eased themselves from my body, the light around me was actually the right temperature. There was just this really great feeling about it. It felt like clean fresh sheets straight from the dryer. I just sunk into the comfort of the light. Then with the passing of each breath I began to think about everything. My childhood, that one time at band camp, my family, conch salad, the fact that I needed an oil change, Bruno Mars' first album...etc., just all sorts of stuff. As I became more at ease, I looked over at the man again and he was looking back at me. His eyes were like dark brown marbles, yet bright at the same time. He had a pleasant face for an older man. His beard was full, tamed and seasoned with grey strands. And that smile of his, seemed to be a permanent expression on his face. The longer I stared at him, his dark, shiny eyes began to draw me in more. I had succumbed to the lures of the glow. And while my body and mind had calmed, I just knew that this was the perfect moment for him to pierce his fangs into my jugular and my soul would be eternally damned. But as we continued to gaze at one another a small light appeared before our eyes. It was… it was beautiful! It was golden-ish and bright, but not too bright. There were these symbols that shimmered within it… and it even felt alive! Then the man's voice was in my head… "Welcome" he said. "I had the same look on my face, when it happened to me", he chuckled. "I am Elegua, son of Ogun and Oya. I am descendant of your Elohii heritage and was sent to help guide your destiny. I am Lord of doorways and righteous paths and you my dear, have been summoned to begin your journey. I know you have many questions and I have their answers. The light before us is the Amore. It is the cosmic line of blessings and protection sent directly from Giza. The Amore is the literal and physical manifestation of our Goddess Pisim, Anh Sang and the Am source. It is their maternal love that watches over our ancestry, our people. The Amore is known by your generation as a spiritual connection. It is what keeps us and our Gods connected."

As Elegua narrated visions from the Amore, the light before us, showed me the tale. I saw, witnessed rather, so many moments. The Amore took me to a moments before and through time where mighty beings created the cosmos and pretty much everything. Catching only a flash of Elegua's lifetime, I saw him sacrificed to save his mother and father. He was torn in half by foreign rulers Malice the First Son and his pair Mentira. They along with their descendants, the Eliite had wreaked havoc upon Elegua's village. He was granted with the decree of Awareness. His duty was to help some of our very first ancestor's transition into his lifetime. Because of his willingness to die for those he loved, he was made God of destiny and fate. After seeing brief moments of Elegua's transition, I was transported further and deeper into the portal. As I sat there staring into the vision, Elegua told me to focus. "Here is where you must focus… not on the darkness behind your eyes but the light that shines within. Here is where you listen to the truth within your silence. Do not think of anything and do not focus on anything but allow yourself to become centered without concentrating on it." I found his instructions hard to follow, but with the ease of this light around me and the calmness of the trance, his instructions were weirdly clear. He continued, "forget what you know. Attach your mind and spirit to nothing yet allow yourself to engage with everything. Who are you Leslie? Are you spirit? Are you flesh? Are you both? Are you neither? Is your spirit designed specifically to fit your form? "or" could it dwell elsewhere? And… what about your flesh! What will happen when it ceases to exist? What or who will you become? Do not think of yourself but become yourself. Listen to the truth of your silence and see the light of your darkness."

As I engaged with myself, without trying to engage…Elegua's voice soon faded away, then there was just me. The Amore must've placed me so far under her glow because it was officially dark. I mean I could not see myself, nor a shadow, nor any source of light. I also could not hear, not the breeze, not my fingers snapping nor the whispers of any life, not even my own. I was in complete darkness and total silence. I waited and waited and waited… then waited some more, until finally, something. Within this absence of light and sound where I floated, a tiny speck of light appeared. It was so minimal, that it was barely there. It could not compare to the amount of darkness that surrounded it. But I somehow knew that this was the exact moment I'd been waiting for. The presence of this very tiny, very minuscule light began to shine. First, flickering as if it had to learn to stay lit. Then the shine became consistent, but still sporadic. It eventually took some time, but it began to shine brighter. As it stayed lit, it began to grow like a sun making its way to high noon. It became so bright that it drowned the absence with its radiance. This lovely brightness once large enough insisted upon the Infinity's dark and quiet essence, swaying, and flowing freely. Her soft and steady tunes interrupted the Infinitude's silence. Although, he did not have a sound like the light, his dark form emerged tall and confident, planting himself in front of the glow. Upon this initial meet, I could not hear specific words, but somehow understood enough to know that she was the **Am** and he the **Infinite**. Although existing within the same eternity as Infinitus, the Am aged into existence. She grew within the Infinitude then emerged once matured. She is part of the first source, and Infinitus' equal. They both were thee sources of all existence.

As his strength towered over her, the Am fluttered an array of colorful sounds as he stood near her. Prior to the Am's presence, the Infinitude was forever silent and forever without light. Quiet and dark since always. It was the Am's presence that awakened him. As they continued to examine one another with curiosity, like an awkward first date, the Infinity eagerly wrapped his aura around the Am. His silence and pitch-black darkness completely surrounding the Am. And once again, I was back in the dark. But surprisingly, the Am's presence grew louder and brighter. She didn't seem to be phased by his size or stillness, for she had might as well. She toyed with him by spinning and moving all around him, like if she could not help but dance to the sounds of the light she produced. Their sources soon eclipsed one another. Fading between light and darkness; sound and silence… then…a blinding explosion erupted, and a tremendous percussion pounded throughout this void where I was… its glow grew larger and brighter, revolving faster and faster. It reminded me of my heartbeat when I was freaking out…thump thump, THUMP THUMP!!! Their combined energy exploded. The eruption of fluid separated into four independent masses as Infinitus and the Am disappeared. As these masses shifted and spiraled and twisted around as if they were trying to find the right fit, each mass finally settled. As they took shape, they resembled what I knew to be continents. One mass was wet black and shaped like Africa. Then another mass was without any color, it looked like white marble and shaped like Europe. The two final forms once settled were a golden yellow and shaped like Asia and the other mass was like an emerald color and shaped like America. After taking these shapes, they laid still for what felt like hours. Then the four masses awakened and solidified into full being like figures. The black and white figures took on masculine forms while the golden yellow and green figures took on feminine forms. Once again, I could not hear words being spoken, but I somehow understood that these giant beings were the heirs of Infinity and Am, better known as... **Creators**.

2. Creators

The Infinitude's absence of light and sound produced the force Giza and Okotadi, brothers and equal parts of the dark and silent energy.

Giza was the cosmic Creator of organic minerals, liquids, jewels, stone, soils, and clay. He was the foundation and mass of organic planets and the flesh of organisms. He was part of the masculine source, the physical presence and strength of beings. He possessed the power to build and contain life.

Okotadi was the cosmic Creator of logic, possibilities, and realities. He spoke with calculation and precision. He was part of the masculine source, the intellect and science of the organic planets and organisms built by his brother. He possessed the power to animate and sustain life.

The Am's presence of light and sound produced the goddess Pisim and Anh Sang, sisters and equal parts of the light and sonic energy.

Anh Sang was the cosmic Creator of reason and balance. She was part of the feminine source, the perfections and precisions of the multiverses and their realms. She possessed the power of knowledge and was Okotadi's equal.

Pisim was the cosmic Creator of nature. She was part of the feminine source, the emotional state of the cosmos and all beings. She possessed the power of growth and love and was Giza's equal.

Their story begins, within the realms of Origen...

3. Origen

"Hmmm…maybe a bit of stone". As Anh Sang exhales the air before her becomes stone … "Now let's give it a neutral carbonated exterior…control of the gravitational properties…yes", she murmurs. "Let's set to 19C." The elements emerged, gathered, and formed into a planetoid. As Anh Sang continues creating, she sensed her sister's energy approaching her realm… Pisim enters curiously… "Are those rings of gravitational polarity, within its seasonal structure?" Resembling the true tone of a big sister. Anh Sang smiles and with a gentle tone, speaks. "Oh, sister, you worry! The gravitational polarity was better placed on the surface of the planetoid, compelling the seasons to last a generation at a time." Pisim to Anh Sang, "what will you name her?" Anh Sang glances at the planetoid, pauses, and says, "Artemai and she will be birthed of strength and beauty" … Anh Sang inquires… "Your peace is minimal sister, explain?" Pisim, exhales sorrowfully and as her breath waved across the realm light rain fell upon Anh Sang's planetary lesson. Pisim followed the rain and approached Anh Sang as she begins to add weather and seasons to Artemai. "I have witnessed more creation happening between Giza and Okotadi" … Anh Sang, not comprehending "I remain unclear, we all have created together." Pisim finding it uneasy to explain, so she recalls the memory. As they both watch Giza and Okotadi combine their essence over the course of generations, Anh Sang is oblivious in understanding matters of emotion. Anh Sang was more passionate about creating and discovering. Pisim, lightly speaks… "Giza and I have not created for an Eon now, but he seems quite interested to create with Okotadi." Pisim's light began to sadden. Anh Sang could not understand her sister's dimness, but suggested she attempts once more, when Okotadi is not around. Pisim grew bright, embraced her sister, then evaporated to the tertiary corner of Origen to request an audience with Giza. As Pisim condensed into her brother's realm, she noticed Okotadi serially watching Giza. Nervously, yet assertively she calls Giza, "My Equal… I would love to share with you for a moment." Okotadi glances over at Pisim and attempts to speak… but Pisim interrupts before he has the chance, "Giza is to whom I speak, Okotadi." He politely smiles and says, "But of course sister" and removes himself, then quietly stalked from a neighboring realm. Pisim begins… "It's been an Eon", Giza obliviously, "an Eon since?" … Pisim attempting to remain bright… "It has been an Eon since, we've created, since we've loved." Giza… "Not possible, we created …" he draws a blank as he attempts to recall the last time, he and Pisim created and says "possible? … brother and I have been manifesting our potential, that it did not appeal to me the distance between you and I." Pisim, "it was foolish for me to bother." Giza patiently saying, "not at all, please come. Let me show you what we've done." Okotadi attentively listening and watching Giza, "brother and I call them constellations, and this group of stars, galaxies. We are building …actually, let us visit." Giza guides Pisim to the master planetoid. A place of peace and creatures and science. Not believing the wonders before her, Pisim flutters different shades of color out of her excitement. Giza glanced at her form, impressed by her radiance and joy. Giza almost forgot what he wanted to show her.

Pisim: What shape is the planetoid?

Giza: A cubical. Okotadi stated that the shape of the planetoid mattered if the inhabitants would have biological perspectives of their reality. He's calculated for the potential of perspectives.

Pisim: Extraordinary! Brother is beyond our intelligence.

Giza: Brother's logic is exceptional… perfect!

As they both admired their surroundings. Giza marvelously says, "She is Origen", Pisim looked around at this planet filled with exotic beauties and marveled at paradise. Amazing beasts roamed across this planet in pairs of male and female types. Structures and mountains and streams and plant life all coexisted harmoniously. The planet honored the Creators with sunshine in the days and bowed for an equal time in the nights. Pisim's celestial form turned to randomized gradients of reds and yellows, violets, and oranges. Excitedly she granted the master planet her grace. Light rain and cool days were now forever upon Origen. Giza, excited by Pisim's vibrantly hued form became intoxicated, just as the absence of light was intrigued by the Am's presence of light, during the first beginning. "Oh, my equal, how beautifully you exist" as he gazes at her and becomes consumed. Giza reaches for Pisim and draws her near to him. She willingly responds. Giza embraces Pisim gently. The pounding of thunder echoed throughout the paradise as the skies set to dusk, and the cool breeze engulfed them both. Giza stood proud before Pisim as he imposed against her pulsating form. Pisim's echoing aura waved across the multiverse, as she and Giza merged. Thunder and lightning blazed through the realms. As Okotadi intently watched Giza and Pisim intertwined within one another he became enraged. Okotadi drastically relocated to his quadrant dimension near Cancer's moon, where he paced and moaned to himself, "How could she, intrude! We created! Us! … How dare she!" Anh Sang approached as she sensed her equal's troubled kinesis. "Of what do you speak?" Okotadi tries to adjust his temperament, but is so consumed with anguish and disappointment thus could not modify his disposition…

Okotadi: Pisim interrupted our creating!

Anh Sang: You rather enjoy creating with brother

Okotadi: We were developing advancements and creatures, something simply amazing. Then she arrived, full of color and joy

Anh Sang: Pisim and Giza have not created for over an Eon, how much more distance shall you demand from her?

Okotadi's emotions bolted through his eyes as Anh Sang defended her sister's reason. Okotadi, instantly perturbed, evaporates, leaving Anh Sang confounded by his energy. Anh Sang has never felt anything like it and was intrigued behind its presence.

Giza and Pisim spent a few more decades within the planet than intended. Together they created biosystems and ecosystems in many parts of the regions. Giza placed marble, lapis lazulis, quartz, golden and ivory tar within the anatomy of the planet. Coal and diamonds all throughout her structure, empowering her life-sustaining energy. Sapphire trees stood proud with plumage and orchids. A paradise unique in its design. There were valleys and canyons, lakes, rivers, and jungles of plenty. The creatures of the planet were sustained from the lands and the lands were happy. Okotadi intently stalked his Creator kin throughout the centuries, for he'd became immensely jealous. Lurking about, his moments unconsciously rendered to witness upon Giza and Pisim. As he walked upon the lands with contempt, Okotadi was unaware of his ills and obsessions. His efforts to remain positive vanished and he'd sunken into a lustful reality of himself creating with Giza to elevate his knowledge, to elevate his potential.

Once upon a day as Okotadi stalked about Anh Sang approached him, "My equal, may I request a moment with you?" Okotadi did not respond. He had not even noticed Anh attempting to communicate with him. Anh Sang, repeated, this time projecting her voice louder… "Tadi, may I request a moment?" Okotadi did not answer, Anh Sang intrigued by his altered state. She had detected the change in his character for some time but was now eager to comprehend it. Okotadi, engulfed in his watch, did not notice Anh Sang observing him. As she circled around him examining him from head to toe, through his aura and form. She noticed the essence upon his heel had darkened. His gaze unbothered by his surroundings. Once Anh Sang observed and collected enough data, she extended her hand to Okotadi, instantly removing his fantastical reality. Disrupted from his desire, he immediately altered his demeanor, and as he intended to speak.

Anh Sang interrupted, "there's no need. For, I only wish to comprehend. Your energy is different from any we become."

Okotadi: You wish to comprehend! Do you really Anh? Want to know how I have comprehended and experienced a lifetime consumed by this…this…this feeling! A feeling which I cannot compute! One that I cannot alter, nor dispose of! These possibilities are inconclusive! And you merely wish to… comprehend, as if it were explicable. I…am…maddened… Giza and I created wonders! Diluting and transferring waves of life forces. Making Origen and her universe and organisms unlike any other, because together Giza and I are power! We are logic, we are complete! We are finite! I desire to create and remain whole. It is my nature to seek precision, to demand perfection! Giza's potential and existence parallels mine. We challenged and evolved in understanding. But now he has betrayed my knowledge! Origen was created by Us Anh, Us! Pisim walks about part my creation as if it were her own. Marking it with her weather and seasons of…feelings (disgustingly).

Anh Sang: I am unable to comprehend your irrationality. You have become unlike us, but what beguiles my thoughts, is why?".

Okotadi: (With dismay) If I were to dismantle all your theories, all of your formulaic properties and could not nor would I return them as created, what would become of you? How would your logic deal?

As Okotadi moved closer to Anh, she sensed his energy flare, and it grabbed her curiosity. She fancied analyzing dynamics and Okotadi's nature excited her desire to observe, record and experiment. Okotadi, attempted to lure Anh Sang to create, but fails.

Anh Sang: Creating at this moment will interrupt my intrigue and thus distract my new formulated thoughts. Perhaps, two eons from the next eclipse would be more beneficial to my timeframe.

Agitated by her rejection, Okotadi evaporated and continued to his lurking.

As two eons from the next eclipse emerged Anh Sang completed thinking about Okotadi's kinesis. She then set to attract her equal. For she knew, logically that she needed to create with Okotadi, given their attraction to one another. However, upon entering his realms she realized he was not himself. Anh Sang was curious to understand why a change in form, but she notices, that Okotadi's gaze is fixed upon Pisim and Giza as they engage in the dance of creation upon Origen, as they often do. However, this time something was different. Okotadi's ill probabilities and physics had slowly altered the environment. Many of the natural orders had begun to shift. As Giza and Pisim concluded their dance, seasons swept across the lands bringing the planet to full bloom. Pisim then noticed a change within Origen and after a few days, two figures emerged from the grounds and laid upon the soil in stillness. Giza and Pisim stood over these pods. They noticed one pod contained a form that was masculine and the other feminine. Pisim spread the sun's warmth over them. As the forms lay upon the earth they made no sound, nor did they move.

Pisim then placed clouds to shower over them. As the forms grew their pod shed a layer each day. On the 7th day the rain stopped. The surrounding form cracked and crumbled back into the ground. **Adunai** arose and stood strong and tall. His eyes opened, his breaths steady and deep. As Adunai gained awareness, he noticed Giza and Pisim standing over him. Pisim stood before him inspecting his type. Although he was not of the night skies like Giza, he resembled him. His skin was rich like the soil, his teeth made of Ivory minerals that Giza had placed into Origen. Gold flowed through his body as charcoal-gems shined for eyes. Astound by his design, Giza felt a sense of joy beyond his normal understanding. Giza blew his grace upon Adunai, crowning his heir most high of the lands. As Adunai inhaled the breath given unto him by Giza, he had become fully in tune with his existence, then kneeled before Giza and Pisim. Before Giza could approach Adunai, the feminine figure emerged from her pod as it crumbled back into the ground as well. **Inaru** was a different type then Adunai but composed equally to him and her beauty resembled that of her mother Pisim. She too was golden inside with moons for eyes. Her form was bright and warm like the fires of Origen and her hair stood out as if it was reaching for the sun. Pisim, blew her grace upon Inaru, crowning her heir most high of the lands. Inaru inhaled the breath given unto her by Pisim, she had become fully in tune with her existence, then kneeled before Giza and Pisim.

The two figures were born of the master planetoid, but from the love of Giza and Pisim. Okotadi, enraged, withdrew from the tree, and became whole in form once again. He appeared before his brother and intensely, "WHAT IS THIS" ... as steam dispensed from his nostrils. "I have watched, and I have waited... and you have forgotten about my existence!"

Giza: Brother! You must witness

Okotadi: Oh, I've witnessed (in utter disgust). I've witnessed for centuries, your betrayal.

Giza: Betrayal? ... I know not what you mean

Okotadi: (Mocking Giza and sneering) You know not what I mean... of course you know not what I mean...your lack of interest to continue what we started is what I mean!

Giza: But Pisim required me, and I willingly submitted. She and I have created a wonder unlike any other. Please brother do not be ill. They are constructed from the very planetoid that we created. They are just as much of you as they are of us.

 Okotadi was consumed by his uneasiness, for what seemed a lifetime, but as always, Giza's pleasantness always brings him peace. Before continuing with his contempt, he took a moment to study these new forms. He assessed their mechanics and rational biology. He was intrigued at how both types resembled Giza and Pisim, yet their form and perspectives mirrored that of Origen. His curiosity slowly outweighed his scorn. He was suddenly amazed by these creatures and wanted to know more of them.

With a great inhale and exhale, Okotadi regained his peace, "forgive my weakness, for I miscalculated the situation."

Giza: No need for forgiveness brother, you are my joy (as he reaches out to Okotadi and places his hand upon his shoulder). We will continue our works and introduce the heirs to their land. There is never a need for you to become uneasy, for we are always, and the heirs are a part of our All.

Although the Creators were Gods, during the very first beginning they had to learn how to become. Their abilities to create and reshape were everlasting traits, but there was still so much they needed to learn. The heirs on the other hand were not bound by the same eternity and limitlessness as the Creators. Their arrival brought about change. During Okotadi's fury, he altered the chemistry upon the planet, thus slightly weakening the balance that existed. Consumed by his obsession he hadn't realized the changes and the effects to the environment. He hadn't calculated for these possibilities nor studied the forces as he had once done. The heirs were born of the adjusted lands and subjected to a life unknown to any other organism ever created.

4. Ombalance

The presence and newness of the heirs brought forth a new cycle to Origen. The atmosphere appealed to their existence. The days had become shortened, creating days and nights, allowing the heirs to rest their forms. The seasons were altered, keeping up with the growth cycle of the heirs. The seasons then became an element in the blossoming of various foods for their consumption. The male, Adunai spent many of his days with Okotadi. He took an interest in the various types of sciences behind the planet's intelligent forces. Particularly to that of the beasts and their natural habitats. Adunai was amazed at the way life somehow knew what to do. Adunai would spend much time conversing with the grounds, so much that in the presence of the young god the mountains would bow. Okotadi took such a liking to Adunai and even more to the mechanics of his being. He noticed how the heirs' needed to breathe, eat and rest. Okotadi became occupied with analyzing Origen's changes along with the heirs. The planet too was influenced by her offspring. She knew to provide their foods, air, and water. Okotadi was in constant observation of Adunai and Inaru but was most fascinated with time as it was now a catalyst of their existence.

The female, Inaru resembled her mother. She too, was a free spirit who loved nature. She would swim and play with the water beasts constantly. The air creatures sang with her in the wake of the days and serenaded the lands alongside her in the evenings. The heiress was clever as she was lovely. She could control the particles to create weather like her mother and articulate the physics of the surrounding forces like her aunt Anh Sang. She met with them daily to learn. Both Adunai and Inaru were blessed and very much loved by the Creators.

Upon a day, Okotadi was in his realm organizing forces for his lesson with Adunai. As he skimmed through his collection of realities, he came across one that made him uneasy. Okotadi watched himself be so consumed with jealousy, he was instantly ashamed and began to terminate the reality, but it would not vanish. He tried again and still could not extinguish the moment. Perplexed, he stood back and widened the scene, entered it, to examine its properties. As he moved through its memory, he found an image so damning he did not know what to do. He allowed himself to live in the moment, during his rage. He had altered his surroundings and the chemistry of the lands. He noticed fruit did not fall from the trees and turn into new trees, but rather perished upon the grounds. He noticed the clouds became dark and heavy prior to the rain falling. Sound waves disappeared from the wind and his footsteps marked the ground beneath him. As he lived within the moment, he attempted to make adjustments but to no avail was unable to alter the moment. As Okotadi continued to examine this possibility, he foresaw that chaos would lay waste to Origen and all that she produced, including the heirs. Molten rock would pour from the mountains and burn all it touched. Plant and Animal types would become carnivorous and devour one another for pleasure, damaging Origen's biology. He immediately withdrew from the moment. With his heart pounding and mind shifting between the images, Okotadi found himself overwhelmed and for the first time fearful. Okotadi gathered his thoughts and began to work on an algorithm. After the passing of several moons, he had not accomplished in finding a solution. He extracted the moment from space and contained it within an astéri, a metalloid-based star, good for hazardous elements.

He then placed the star in the upper galaxy of his realm until he could figure out how to destroy it. Okotadi was ashamed of his creation but knew if the imbalance and time were to somehow combine that the moment would mean catastrophe for the planet and the heirs, for this he could not allow.

Anh Sang enjoyed teaching her goddess about the Cosmo's mechanics. She found it refreshing to explain things to someone for a change, rather than explaining it to one of her multiple versions who already knew as much as she did. Okotadi entered Anh Sang's realm and admired the moment between Anh Sang and Inaru, who seemed to be really intrigued with their lesson.

Inaru: …so, if I'm understanding correctly…centrifugal energy placed at the center of any oxygen-based star, will sprout revolving rings.

Anh Sang: Precisely. But it must maintain a low temperature in its core, or you will get a rotating star rather than circulating rings.

They both laughed on such an irregularity. Okotadi noticed how at ease his equal was and he rather enjoyed watching her not be so rigid as she had once been. It is the same feeling he has when with Adunai.

Okotadi: May I interrupt for a moment

Inaru: Uncle! You must have a look.

Inaru insists, as Okotadi watched Inaru manipulate cosmic properties from young astéri, he knew even more that he needed to destroy his star. He did not want to imagine if she were to manipulate it upon accident. Both Inaru and Adunai were composed of time and the reality would affect them greatly.

Okotadi: That is, wonderful! May I request a moment with my equal.

Inaru: You may

Inaru exits her aunt's realm

Anh Sang: It seems urgent, have you fallen ill again?

Okotadi: During my weakness, I created an inconsistent reality that could devastate Origen and all she produces. I have studied its properties but cannot expire it. If time were to ever combine with this reality…. Oh, I'd rather not say. Will you assist me in finding a solution?

Anh Sang: Something new! Of course, where is the moment?

Okotadi: I've placed it deep within …Scorpion's universe, Volkanis

Anh Sang: What type of destruction will be unleashed, that you had to bury it so deep?

Okotadi: (Ashamed) there would be a shift on moral perception for the organisms and weaken the heart of the planet. But since the heirs were not within the reality, I am unclear as to what will happen to them exactly. Given their delicate biology, they would be subjected to self-destructing attributes… forgive me

Anh Sang: And what will happen to our All?

Okotadi: We will begin to weaken and our all will be subjected to decay… (sorrowfully) as well.

Anh Sang: (Exhales deeply) Then it is time to confront the moment.

Okotadi and Anh Sang appeared in Volkanis to confront the star. As Okotadi revealed the star to his equal, she questioned if she should be the one to retrieve the moment. For it was placed within a star in a galaxy she had created. This seemed logical to Okotadi, and he gave her the star. As she viewed the reality, he explained to her the changes that occurred. Anh Sang was puzzled the All could submit to weakness, for they were the sources of existence. As they both reviewed the moments of Okotadi's weakness...

Anh Sang: Explain to me what you became

Okotadi: I was maddened. Consumed by nothing more than to view my brother's betrayal. I was irresponsible in my actions.

Anh Sang: That I comprehend, but What, were you? ... look here. Your heels scorch the ground beneath you. Your body is slender, and you blend within the branches. The fruit upon the surrounding trees have deteriorated, but you are not your natural form.

Okotadi: I...I was unaware of my form; this form is not any animal we have created.

Anh Sang: Perhaps the property within this beast is distorting the destruction of the reality. We have no calculations of its origin; how can we understand it enough to manipulate its chemistry.

Okotadi: My rage was hungered beyond my control. What shall we do?

Anh Sang: For once I am unsure (as she looked disappointedly at Okotadi). Keep the star here and let us consort with Pisim and Giza.

Okotadi was hesitant about the decision to include the others.

Okotadi: Wait! Perhaps we try a different approach. I feel uneasy showing them such horror.

Anh Sang: I comprehend your apprehension, but there is no time for it. We must remove this possibility; it is much more catastrophic than wounded pride.

Okotadi: Of what you speak is true…

Giza and Pisim sat high above their creations and admired the All's work. As they spoke amongst one another with joy, Okotadi and Anh Sang appeared.

Anh Sang: A moment…

Pisim: Sister, your peace is worried?

Giza: (stood firmly) is it the heirs?

Okotadi: In a matter of speaking…(Exhales) When I grew ill with anger I made changes to the forces within the lands, unknowingly…

Pisim: Changes! What type of changes?

Okotadi: I'd rather allow you to witness

The All appeared upon Volkanis and Okotadi revealed to them the moment contained within the asteri.

Pisim: We were unaware that you were vexed so deeply. Why did you not come speak to us?

Giza: What is your nature brother?

Okotadi: This is the very question we find ourselves unable to answer. The form which I became was not created by us. We believe it is the reason that I am unable to destroy this possibility.

Giza: Why must it be destroyed?

Okotadi: As I further examined the moment, I came to understand that it has the capability of becoming an actuality. Time now exists upon Origen and within the heirs. If it were ever to be unleashed, it will bring about chaos to the mother planet and all she produces.

Giza: Chaos to the mother planet? To the heirs? (He says despairingly)

Okotadi: Forgive me. I was consumed and unaware of my actions.

Pisim: What kind of chaos will be unleashed?

Okotadi: There would be horrible changes to the life forces of the planet. The moral perception of the organisms will weaken. I am unclear as to what will happen to Adunai and Inaru, but they will be subjected to self-destructing attributes as well (Embarrassed looking at Giza and Pisim) we All will weaken, and our creations will decay over generations.

Giza and Pisim were speechless, they could not understand why this was happening nor why Okotadi would be maddened to such depths.

For he knew well enough Giza and Pisim are equaled forces, just as he and Anh Sang.

Giza: Forgiveness you have my brother. I know this was not what you intended. From what I understand you unleashed an imbalance upon the land and upon us as well. We must come together and produce a balanced reality and place the moment within it. Then we can vanquish that reality.

Anh Sang: Yes! We need to make the reality eons or perhaps infinite, providing the chaos enough space to cancel or exhaust itself, then when weakened, we can destroy the reality.

Pisim: Will this work?

Giza: We must try until it does. Is there anything else we need to know Okotadi, before attempting?

Okotadi: If we fail and cannot destroy nor contain the chaos, it will spread throughout and even, beyond time.

Pisim: What do you suggest?

Okotadi: Create another planetoid, like the mother, but without time and unleash it there and let the chaos loose, trapped within a loop of reality, it will eventually destroy itself and the planet.

Anh Sang: Destruction!... of a mother planet!?

Okotadi: From what I have calculated, it is the only way. Once unleashed we may not be able to place it within the star and if it attaches to time, we risk mother being infected, along with the heirs.

The news faded Pisim to randomized shades of blues and grays, for she had become saddened at the idea.

Giza: What if we destroyed the star, or this quadrant in which it resides?

Okotadi: There are no life forces, thus no possibilities. It will continue to exist after the planet is gone. It has to remain looped outside of time and it will eventually cancel itself.

The Creators decided to create another mother planet to sacrifice unto the imbalance. The form which Okotadi had become was chaos, a force the All never encountered nor could ever predict. It was a force of consumption, darkness, and misunderstanding.

Inaru: Something new! (Spoken like her aunt, who is constantly intrigued by learning) May we visit Volkanis, mother?

Origen: You may my darlings…You must be back to your lands by the settling of the evening sun.

Inaru and Adunai bowed before the mother, in acceptance of her order.

Inaru: Anh Sang has been teaching me to manipulate the stars and I will demonstrate for you.

Inaru walks off in confidence, while Adunai smiles at her goofiness.

As they enter Volkanis, Adunai notices the grounds were hard yet powdery at the same time. Adunai speaks to the grounds, but these did not respond, they were silent. This made him feel uneasy, for he has not encountered lands that could not speak.

Adunai: Odd… the lands are not awoken

Inaru: No, it is a volcanic region, and the lands are carbonic particles, essentially soot.

Adunai: Soot? What an odd word (as he chuckles at the word and then repeats) Soot!

Inaru: O brother… come I have learned to manipulate the energy within the stars. I can change their shine or make them bigger. I can even add rings to them. Which shall I do first? (excitedly)

Adunai: Look at that star. Can you make it brighter?

Inaru approaches the star with curiosity. The dimness captured her attention.

Inaru: Hmm… I can make this brighter, but it appears that there is something within this star. It is very different than any dark matter within a star that I've seen. In fact, I was under the impression I had seen them all.

Adunai: Mother why does this appear so?

Origen was unable to commune with the heirs, for the looseness of the soot she could not comprehend.

Adunai: Mother?

Inaru: You cannot speak to her from here, the lands are not organic like her

Adunai: I am not fond of this place. It disturbs my aura. Let us go it will be dusk soon.

Inaru: We have barely explored our potential here. As Inaru reached for the asteri with the least brilliance…

Adunai interrupts

Adunai: It is time, we must leave

Inaru finding it hard to look away, but she does, and they return to their lands.

Origen: Did you learn much?

Inaru: There is the most peculiar bleakness of the stars there. I will have a closer look when we awaken.

Origen: You are very curious

Adunai: Where are the All? I have never known them to be scarce

Origen: They are deep in creation; this is the only time their presence is vague.

As the following morning approaches, the air fowls serenade the sun to rise and Inaru jumps up with excitement. She was still intrigued and planned to study the stars of Exodus. First, she meets with the animals and plants of the lands as she does every day. It is after she has completed her duties, that she is in a hurry to return to the planet.

Inaru: Brother…will you accompany me back to Volkanis?

Adunai: I do not care for that land (as he lazily rides on the back of Adon the male Leo.)

Inaru: Aren't you interested in learning as much as possible?

Adunai: The land there disturbs me…the soot (smilingly) is incoherent, why would I want to learn about it?

Inaru: Will you accompany me to the planet, I choose to explore?

Adunai's uneasiness did not stop Inaru, her hunger for learning and absorbing new information was grand.

Adunai: I will accompany you…just for a while. I had planned on spending the day with Adon.

As the heirs set for Volkanis, the All were just completing the new mother planet in a fractional quadrant. They had to create the planetoid deep within eternal space, so it would not interrupt Origen or anything within her universe.

Pisim: She is phenomenal…her destiny saddens me.

Giza: I understand your love (as he caresses Pisim's face), but we must stop any imbalances from occurring. Think of our heirs…

As Okotadi stares upon the planet he measures the different dynamic forces, while Anh Sang recalculates its equations. He nods in approval, the time to retrieve the possibility and unleash it has arrived.

Okotadi: Before we introduce the moment, what shall we name her?

Giza: A name serves no relevance, rather we seek her forgiveness. Look at how wondrous she is.

Giza sighs, looks at Okotadi and says, "It is time." The All gather and begin to travel to retrieve the star.

Meanwhile…As Inaru makes her way to the star, Adunai's aura begins to tense him. He becomes uneasy upon the planet's surface.

Adunai: Inaru! I cannot be here; my presence is touched by the lifelessness here.

Inaru was under an intrigued stare. She ignores Adunai and appears on top of the star. As she looks inside, she is completely taken over. Adunai intently calls for Inaru, but she is possessed by the components within the star. Adunai moves toward Inaru and becomes slightly ill. He is flushed in color, his rich black hue, becomes depressed and opaque. His steps become heavy. His breathing becomes harder. As he struggles to walk over, he looks down at his feet. Adunai notices the soot marking his feet. The soot began making its way up his legs. Adunai began to panic, he felt the weight of the soot pulling him down. He attempts another step, in hopes to grab Inaru, but fails at both. Adunai yells, "Mother!!!", but she does not reply. Adunai nearly to the ground calls for Inaru once more. He gathers his breath and unleashes a yell so powerful that his voice trembles the planet and Inaru's gaze. As she comes to, turns to her brother, and sees him in pain and flashes over to his aid…

Inaru: Brother…how did…what has happened to you?

Adunai: This place weakens me (he pants slowly). It seeks to destroy me!

Inaru: Then we must leave, immediately!

Before the heirs could leave Volkanis the moment contained within the star had become a part of Inaru's reality. As she engaged with the star her presence collided with fragments of the chaos. As Inaru helps Adunai up, she falls to the ground unconsciously. Adunai struggled with gathering his sister and forcing them beyond these foreign lands. But he gathers his strength and painfully exerts them back to the lands of Origen they knew. The planet becomes immediately aware of their pain.

Adunai: Mother! Mother!

Origen: What has happened!? You both feel…you both feel…

Origen was perplexed and unable to explain the agony radiating from Adunai…for it was an unknown substance. She is stunned that the heirs had both fallen ill and she did not know the cause. Upon the All's arrival, they noticed the shift in Origen's energy and proceeded to finding the heirs. When they arrived, they witnessed them laying upon the ground.

Origen: They are weakened, but I do not recognize the source.

Okotadi: Where were they weakened?

Adunai gathers a fraction of his strength and with immense fatigue he uttered "Vol…kan" faintly. Okotadi and Giza expired to Volkanis and as they arrive upon the smog infested environment, they witnessed the decaying qualities that spewed from the star. The exterior of the reality was quite lovely as it shimmered like the ocean's surface at dawn, yet its odor was horrid and grotesque. It reeked of pain, heat, and wrath. As its putridity spread, it obliterated all it touched. Giza could not believe that such a source existed. He gathered nearby palms, boulders, and gems, hurling them at Volkanis, but they disbursed into ash matter as they neared its sick aura. Okotadi's stare was fixed upon the chaotic ooze. The longer he looked upon it the more he began to feel uneasy. His body began to recall the emotions that created such an energy. His gaze became locked. He stood in complete stillness. The reality which he feared appealed to him, slowly making its way toward him. Okotadi's hands began to tremble, his eyes mimicked the reflection of the ooze as his form slowly thinned. Volkanis' environment became unstable and started to melt. After Giza's efforts to destroy the destruction failed, he noticed his brother in a still stance. "Brother", he called out to him, but Okotadi did not move. Giza stood in front of Okotadi, and as he looked in his eyes, he sensed an unfamiliar presence within him. Giza broke Okotadi's stare by placing him within his source, then leading them both back to the mainland. When they reached mother's land Okotadi looked upon Giza with pain and fear, then whispered…

Okotadi: Brother, I am fearful

Giza not fully understanding the imbalance but knew that Okotadi was the source. He took Okotadi and surrounded him with his peace until he regained strength.

Giza: Brother…are you with me?

Okotadi inhales deeply and slowly comes to…

Okotadi: Yes…yes, I believe I am all here. Thank you, Giza!!!

As they returned to see the heirs, Adunai seemed to be fighting with its consumption while Inaru was completely unconscious. Pisim wrapped Adunai in her aura for stabilization. Anh Sang joined her as they engulfed him with their light and low healing frequency. They then placed him within the soils of Origen for restoration. But to revive Inaru, the power of the All was required. Once Adunai was safely cocooned within the soils of Origen, both Anh Sang and Pisim attempted to restore Inaru, just like they had done with the male heir.

But their light was not sufficient. They wrapped the female heir in their source, but the following attempts failed. Giza and Okotadi, noticing Inaru's immovable state, thus blended with their equals. Never performing such an act of restoration, light, sound, and the absence of light and sound from the original sources attached to her essence without the Creators' awareness. Fully exposed Inaru arose gracefully. She exited the portal with poise and strength. As the All's essence surrounded her, Inaru had become reborn. She was now endowed with knowledge from the original source. As the presence and absence grew within Inaru, the direct connection to the beginning and the ending had now infused with time itself. Rather than appearing weakened like her brother, she emerged from within its portal, as if unaffected, by the chaos. To see her feeling better eased most of the tension, but Okotadi's weakness perplexed Giza. He did not want to confront him until they had come up with a solution to contain the chaos from spreading.

In the days to follow, the Creators examined the heirs thoroughly. Where they found Adunai to be as he was, Inaru however, showed an increase in her potential. She no longer slept and ate with Adunai. Most of her time was spent with Pisim and Anh Sang configuring solutions to dissolve the chaos. Out of curiosity for her increased potential Okotadi examined Inaru from a distance. However, in his obsession to retrieve new data from Inaru, he was unaware of Giza observing him from afar. Giza was concerned not to bring the imbalance upon the mother planet, but he worried that it lived within his brother.

6. Fallen

Many seasons had passed as the poisoned reality inched its way through time…slowly… approaching the present day of Origen's universe. Although the imbalance had been released, it's physiology needed time to mature. This flaw granted the Creators an opportunity to find a solution. As the seasons passed small changes within Origen's biology had begun to shift. Her days had become shorter and hotter, her winters became unbearable for many of the inhabitants. The air fowl and land beasts took refuge within the mountains and plants of the lands. Okotadi studied the seasons, terrain, and waters, attempting to account for all anomalies. He carefully adjusted the equations to many of the organisms, restoring the order to their cycles. He was confident that he would eventually find the correct calculation to balance and stop the chaos. The heirs had become of much assistance, they tended to the lands and animals, while also collecting data and monitoring changes to aid in finding a solution. For the past six decades, this had been the focus and thus the overall goal of the Creators and the heirs. During this time Inaru's dynamic changed exponentially. She had become stronger than Adunai and more like the Creators. Her potential broadened.

As Adunai strolled upon the land with Adon his Leo he noticed one day, Inaru standing in stillness. Her gaze locked upon the skies above her. As she stood there with her body firm, Inaru evaporated. Adunai, shocked as he was unaware that they possessed the ability to move as the lords. Adunai stood around and waited for her to reappear, but she did not. As he later returned to his dwellings she was there, examining particles of a peculiar plant.

Adunai: What is it?

Inaru: It is a cannabidiol fern. I am measuring it's healing qualities.

Adunai: From where does it come?

Inaru: The edge of our universe has smaller planets made from the most peculiar vegetation and plant life. It is most beautiful. You should accompany me on the next visit...

Adunai: How am I to get there, I do not evaporate as you do

Inaru: I can teach you

Adunai: How?

Inaru: After we had fallen ill from Volkanis, I emerged feeling new. I began to see things clearly and with more intensity

Adunai: What do you mean?

Inaru: I believe I am becoming a Creator, Dune. I can do much of what the All can... my potential has gained momentum. I can see into the voids and quadrants of this multiverse... and wherever I set my gaze, is where I evaporate, I can exist anywhere and anytime.

Adunai: This cannot be. They...they Created us; we are of this land... we belong to them!... we have limits!?

Inaru: Peace Adunai. I can sense how this must confuse you, but... I feel...more! I know more! I am... more! Your limitations no longer apply to me. Limits no longer apply to me Dune, nor should they to you my love, my friend, my brother, my peace...

As she says these words to him, Inaru approaches Adunai slowly, yet confidently. Her gaze fixed upon his strength and his beauty. She hears the pounding of his heart. Also noticing the increased stream of his golden essence flowing within his form. Inaru reads the awkward curiosity upon his face, yet his energy is alluring. Inaru's desires bolted through her form. The static excited her hair as it gravitated outward toward the skies.

Inaru: Do not fear me Adunai... we were made to be more. To sustain more. I am yours and you are mine... haven't you examined life? All the mother planet produces is as we are, is as the Creators are. One male and one female, balance. These forces coexist to maintain order and produce life forces. Please do not fear me, Dune.

Adunai was captivated by Inaru's presence. His senses dulled as an inner hunger grew. He looked into her eyes as waves jolted through them and for the first time, he sensed desire. Never feeling this emotion before he felt the need to ask Origen what was happening to him. However, Adunai was unable to remove his gaze and speak. He shortly found himself placing his arms around Inaru. Her form was delicate, and she smelled of the citrus groves during sunset. Her eyes shined like the frozen gems of the mountaintops. Her beauty was overwhelming Adunai, for he could not refrain from placing his lips upon hers while caressing her waves. Inaru pulled him closer. Their energies and bodies slowly engaged into the dance of creation. The ground beneath them shook throughout all of Origen.

Supposedly the Creators could engage in the forever dance, for the heirs were not meant to, nor should they have had knowledge of its existence and purpose. However, Inaru's exposures to the unstable energy from within the star in combination with the All's source, bestowed upon her a Creator-like insight. As they fused, the lands changed along with Origen's form. The edge of the cubed planet rounded, as her waters spread fiercely about the planet, splicing many of the lands away from one another. Mountains sunk into the oceans and lakes, trees split and fell into the pits of the planet along with many animals. As the All made it to the heirs, Giza knew they were too late, and that chaos had been unleashed from within the heirs and throughout the mother planet. Giza became enraged. His form became pitch black, and his eyes flamed with fire. Pisim demanded the heirs explain themselves.

Inaru: For I have been made aware. I have been able to understand as you All do.

Pisim: Continue

Inaru: When the matter from within the star placed me under its control, I witnessed the end, the destruction of the life and death force. Yet, when under the consumption of the All, I witnessed the beginning and the coming together of the Infinity and the Am. When you restored me, I could sense the same source within you All. Since then, I have become more and now I have shared this with my equal.

Adunai: The presence of the All is within us

Giza: This should not be! We!... are the Creators. You are but mere versions of our love … not more! We are order! We are balance!

Inaru despised the words spoken from her father. Her fury heightened her form as she stood strongly in front of Giza, pulsating in red fiery hues…

Inaru: … not more! Versions?! You speak of us as we are disposable… replaceable! We are more! and will continue to become more! We will it so! This… is the new order, father!

Inaru backed away slowly from Giza, with her gaze attached to his. She grabbed Adunai's arm defiantly evaporating from in front the Creators. In disbelief Pisim turned to Giza, but before she could say a word Giza yelled so powerfully that his voice echoed throughout space. His soundwaves shifted the multiverses. Giza turned his attention to Okotadi, staring silently and sternly at him. Inaru and Adunai vanished to the edge of the universe. Although their power had increased, they were not like the Creators. They could not create worlds and cosmic matter. They were birthed of Origen's lands and limited. However, Inaru was certain that once they reached the completion of their growth cycle that they would become more powerful. They would no longer be heirs of Origen, but gods of Origen.

Adunai: What shall become of us?

Inaru: We wait. We wait until we have fully matured. Let us now seek new dwellings.

As the heirs searched eagerly through space, they finally reached a fractional space in the omni verse. As they entered its atmosphere, they noticed similarities within this new universe. As they approached the lands, they noticed the airs within this quadrant allowed them to keep their current biological composition. They did not need to adapt their forms for survival. The climate suited and sustained them. Inaru and Adunai had found a paradise of new wonders and science energy just like their previous home of Origen. As they roamed about and researched the terrain, they began to make changes to benefit their presence. The animals were given the ability to mate and populate the lands within their order. This freedom was given to the plants as well. The trees provided the same food source they were accustomed to on Origen. Adunai could even speak to the lands. He made their dwellings from the minerals and materials provided by the planet. Adunai reshaped the mountains so he and Inaru could sit above their world. After molding the new planet to their needs and desires, Adunai and Inaru sat upon their mounds, above it all and admired...

Inaru: She is wonderful!

Adunai: She is exquisite! Why is she here all alone and not next to Origen?

The heirs were endowed with such joy and peace. This planet reminded them of their home. Adunai was pleased that their Creators designed such a place for he and Inaru to reign once fully matured.

Adunai: This place is such a blessing; I can feel her breath beneath my feet. Her winds are sweet, and her aura is new. What are you called?

Planet: My Lords did not provide me with a name, simply a function.

Before Inaru could investigate the planet's function Adunai placed his body upon her grounds, rolling around like Adon his Leo, when newly formed. He infused with the environment, sensing her sources, he looks over at Inaru with love and happiness beaming from his eyes...

Adunai: ElohI. Your name now and our children will be the Elohii.

Inaru smiled at Adunai, feeling ever so gracious to feel as one of the Creators.

After the heirs fled, Giza grew stubborn...

Giza: I am not pleased...not pleased at all!

Pisim: Peace Giza. Perhaps it was time for them to belong to one another. Do not be so vexed at their decisions.

As Pisim grabs Giza and looks at him deeply.

Giza: ...There is much to learn about them... and the way she spoke to me! She is strong; however, I will settle for their joy as the sum of their balance... (exhales) shall we appear to them?

Pisim: Give them space, let us see what happens. We will learn of them, and they will teach us of their type. Then we will become better suited to help them and their kind, when needed.

Giza: Do you believe their heirs will make similar decisions?

Pisim: They are limited beings, and although my calculations may not be as accurate as Anh's, they are programmed to follow a biological cycle, we will not constrain their development.

Giza pondered this information and acknowledged that the heirs would need them in due time. The idea calmed Giza's frustration. He parted the air and created a domain where he began to develop elements, he felt the heirs would need, if they ever called upon him. Giza focused his attention upon their land and watched very carefully.

 Meanwhile, upon Origen, Okotadi searched for a solution to the chaos. He wished to rid himself of it, but soon fell to its evils. He had spent much time extracting the poisoned possibilities and placing them within the mountaintop's crystals. The gem's freeze contained the ill. However, as the years passed, the mountain tops became burdened with such madness. The chaos melted the exterior of the gems along with the mountains. The possibilities scorched its insides, creating pits and craters. Wrath and fire bled through it as its boulders absorbed the heat of the flames. Smog dispensed into the air as the winds carried a new form of contempt throughout the atmosphere. Without any awareness Okotadi had become completely maddened. For he had not realized the quantity of irrationalities and irregularities he'd released over the centuries, nor its damages to Origen. The wickedness within the air did not refrain from affecting the animals and the plants. Decay and destruction fell upon the lands. Okotadi's thirst for a solution possessed him. As he stumbled through his thought, he caught a glimpse of the mountain, then suddenly the idea to create a frozen crystal large enough to contain the chaos, appealed to him. He knew it would work but needed Giza's source to construct such a gem. Then it dawned on him, that none of the Creators had been there to aid in the development of his genius.

Okotadi: They are not concerned with ridding the universe of this disaster. They are not concerned. You saw Giza's disappointment (as he spoke to himself). But then again if this works… I would receive credit for its discovery. Then brother would have no choice but to be pleased with my efforts and would forgive all!

As Okotadi quarreled amongst himself, Anh Sang noticed she had not sensed Okotadi's aura for quite some time. In fact, it had been very bleak and hard to notice. As she searched for him and saw that he had fallen ill once more. His form this time had completely changed. It seemed as if what he had thought had taken full shape. Anh Sang hurried to Giza and Pisim and pointed…

Anh Sang: There!

As she pointed in Okotadi's direction the Creators place their attention to Origen, they witnessed Okotadi completely changed. He stood upon the palms of his feet. Sharpened gems protruded from his mouth as his back slumped outward. His form was scorched with symbols and scales while storms brewed inside him. As the Creators watched, they were in disbelief.

Giza: What has he become?

Anh Sang: Unbalanced… Chaos…he breeds it!

Giza: But… I do not understand. How is That… a possibility???

Anh Sang: I have been working on theories since I sensed the flare of his energy. The most logical, is that he is unable to keep his peace without you Giza.

Giza: Without me?

Anh Sang: Precisely! Together you are balanced. He became disturbed when you and Pisim created the heirs. He was alone with his logic for an extended time. Once again, we are here, and he is alone with his logic, and he has completely fallen. He needs balance, he needs peace, Giza. You and he are a balance, as is Pisim and I. Whatever he has become has brought decay to the lands.

Giza: Decay? I shall speak with him. Brother…a moment

As Giza calls out, Okotadi scoffed at the sound of Giza's voice. He was perplexed and uncertain he wanted to include his siblings in his research. As Okotadi ascended to meet with the All, they were shocked at his appearance.

Giza: You are ill brother.

Okotadi: Ill? No, I…I've been working on a solution (oblivious of his appearance)

Giza: It seems that there is no need for a solution. The heirs are balanced and succeeding upon their new planet. Please come join us and restore your peace.

Okotadi appeared bothered. His body was not steady, the presence of light within this realm was too bright for him. His eyes began to burn and his form as well. His insanity telling him that he was sent there to be mocked.

Anh Sang: Is something wrong?

Okotadi: I'm no fool. You want my knowledge! (Breathing heavily) I will not give you the solution…. I will not!!!

Giza: Brother, the chaos is corrupting you. Please let us restore your peace

Okotadi unable to sustain the brightness. His body began to fail him. He fell upon the ground. The scorched markings upon his body burned deeper bringing him much anguish. Okotadi moaned and yelled. Pisim grabbed Okotadi and evaporated with him to Origen.

Once they were back upon the lands his breathing returned to normal. Giza and Anh Sang followed and as they looked upon their lands they were shocked at the destruction. Trees were burnt to ash. The ground was blackened and tough. The air was horrid and many of the animals, extinguished. The once lush and serene paradise was now a barren terrain of putrefying plants, animals, and sanity.

Giza: What happened here (sorrowfully)

Okotadi: What!!! I have tried and tried many forms to control the chaos. I have found that the mountain's crystals hold the poisoned possibilities best.

As they All look upon the mountain tops the peaks were all gone. What remained were hollowed heaps filled of molten rock and despair. Okotadi could not comprehend what had happened to the peaks.

Okotadi: They…I placed them there (confused). You have come to ridicule me, to blame me for THIS!... I…I… have myself to blame, I know. BUT YOU ALL, have taken me for granted. Yes (stumbling over his words). This is…this is my world now. I meant no harm…no harm…I just…I just (he sees them staring at him with amazement, he exhales deeply) …Leave

Giza, Pisim and Anh Sang watched as Okotadi spoke in and out of himself. They were in disbelief. Anh Sang informed Pisim and Giza to leave as she would stay behind to speak with him. After Giza and Pisim departed. Anh Sang turned to Okotadi and says, "teach me". Okotadi looks at Anh Sang with a sinister grin.

Okotadi: You wish to learn? We… can destroy the chaos. I will share this with you, but you must not tell the others (he grazes his talon upon her mouth as to sworn her to secrecy).

Anh Sang: I am concerned about the chaos within you. Teach me how this is possible. Show me, so I can aid in restoring your peace.

Okotadi: Restoring my peace…restore my peace (chuckling). You cannot fool me. You wish to take my knowledge! I am but a method you wish to explore.

Anh Sang: I simply wish to know…

Okotadi approached Anh Sang, circled around her, studying her rhythmic composition for a moment as if she were prey. "Leave", he breathed into her ear, then fled to his realm. As Okotadi looks out upon the nearby galaxy, he mumbles crazily to himself.

Okotadi: Restore my peace, restore MY peace (exhales slowly and heavily) …re..store…p…eace….

An idea jolted through him, and he quickly evaporated to the edge of the universe. As Okotadi sat upon the planet, Hydruus contemplating, he knew that Adunai and Inaru would mature and have heirs of their own and that they would be filled with order and balance. Okotadi thought to himself that he could get the peace he required from them. He could not face Giza, nor did he want to restore with him, but if he could somehow become balanced upon this new world. He and a fully matured Adunai could create the crystal and entrap the chaos to restore Origen. Okotadi knew his plan was excellent and that it would work. In his attempt to head towards ElohI, an odd image startled Okotadi. He did not recognize the reflection before him. It moved about as Okotadi did. The image grinned and winked at him. Instantaneously, it dawned on him that the image was his reflection. He did not recognize himself. As he examined the changes to his form Okotadi realized that it was his unbalanced energy that brought about the destruction. He was able to suddenly recall moments and memories from both himself and his chaotic mind. His tainted exterior was confirmation of it. Rather than continuing his course, he returned to Origen. As he stood and looked out amongst the damages to the mother planet, he had become depressed. He was deeply hurt by his actions. His instability was the reason he could not dwell in perfection with the All and why it pained him to be there. His solution to make everything better faded once he faced his new reality that settled among his thoughts. Tears seeped down his face as Okotadi had no longer worried if the chaos consumed him completely.

7. Orisha

During the time of Adunai and Inaru's reign upon ElohI, they conceived heirs of their own. Men and woman created in the likeness of Origen's Creators. For what had been two centuries upon the new planet, Adunai and Inaru created with pure love all over ElohI. They danced, designed, instilled their will, potential and auras throughout their new universe.

Upon a day Inaru reached a pivot in her weather, showering ElohI's lands with her emotions. Covering the soils, plants, and beings in pure love, joy, and prosperity. After several weeks, earthen pods, like the ones Adunai and Inaru were birthed from grew from the meadows upon ElohI. Arising like stalks of corn, male Elohii and female Elohii had awaken. The Elohii male type arose first, followed by the female type. Uprooting from the essence of nature like flowers in bloom and bringing forth a new cycle of change, a new cycle of life.

These new heirs were known as the **Orishas**, progeny born from ElohI, but created by Adunai and Inaru. They were designed with order and everlasting potential. During their first decade these Elohii, learned much about the Creators of Origen. Adunai thought it important they knew of their beginnings. As Inaru taught her children about the forces within the lands and within themselves. The heirs provided the Orisha with lands according to their likeness.

62

The **Elohii of Giza** inhabited the lands West of the Templo ElohI, the main sanctuary erected by Adunai during years he and Inaru settled onto the planet. The environment was populated with large land and water mammals. Beasts and creatures of all types. The Elohii here were happy and free-spirited beings. They could not make worlds as Giza or reign supreme over the terrain as Adunai, but they tended to the growth and regulations of all the lands on the planet. The **male was called Ogun,** he could manipulate foundational elements such as the soils, stones, and minerals. His specialty were metals, even in their liquid states could he manipulate elements. Ogun had piercing obsidian eyes. He was tall and strong like his father's father. His demeanor was both playful and stealth. His equal and **female was called Oya**, she could manipulate the emotional state of the lands. She was responsible for the blissful seasons but also for its torrential monsoons. Her specialty was that of the spectrum of light and she was just as joyous and stealth as her equal. Both their forms were that of fertile soils and their bones and teeth as the ivory within the bark of the trees. Golden essence surged through them. The Elohii of Giza were the leaders among the Orisha.

The **Elohii of Pisim** were in synch with the weather and happy spirited, as well. The **male was called Cocijo and the female Selu**. They inhabited the lands North of the Templo ElohI and were responsible for balancing and sustaining the plants and vegetation of the land. Selu was an agricultural goddess with a specialty in the maize pods that conceive the Elohii. Cocijo is responsible for providing the right amount of light and sound to ensure their success and growth. They were also responsible for the order of the agriculture for all of the Elohii, which was used for consumption and purification. Their forms were stout and copper. They had bronze stars for eyes as Jade essence flowed through their bodies. They were also lovers of the dance.

The **Elohii of Okotadi** inhabited the Eastern lands beyond the Templo ElohI. The **male was Calyx and female Rhea**. They kept the forces and elements within the lands balanced. They were responsible for the precise temperatures, algorithms, and systems of the entire planet and the Elohii. They were very outspoken and friendly. They constantly walked about the lands discussing how the mechanics of life worked and their causes. They made charts of all the elements and would teach the other Orishas and their progeny. They both lacked pigment, their eyes were made of pearl marble. Golden essence flowed through them just as with the Elohii of Giza. Both Calyx and Rhea were lovers of theory and philosophy.

Lastly, the **Elohii of Anh Sang** inhabited the Southern lands beyond the Templo ElohI. The **male was called Kuei-Shen and the female Hiyori- Li,** and they were responsible for the balance and function of all the animals and animals yet to come. They were quite observant. They found comfort in maintaining their peace and sharing their knowledge. They were bright like the first sun of the day and very playful individuals who loved to laugh. They would design, plan and chart environmental changes. They would often help balance the algorithms and equations with the Elohii of Okotadi. Kuei-Shen 's specialty were the canines of the planet, while Hiyori-Li's specialty were the reptiles. Her pet Komodon, Saturn, followed and kept her company most days. The Elohii of Anh Sang also had Jade essence flowing through their forms.

The first children born of Adunai, Inaru and ElohI, the Orishas collectively used their potentials to maintain the order upon the planet. They assumed their roles with the wake of the first sun and in the rest of the evening moon they came together to share stories, experiences and give thanks to the Creators.

The main sanctuary Templo ElohI, stood above all. This is where the heirs of Origen and their Orishas would gather in the evenings before returning to their dwellings for rest. The sanctuary was large and beautiful. The structure's walls were made of quartz and embroidered with brass. The grounds within the temple paved with various flora jewels that never perished nor blew with the wind. Inside were two thrones besides one another. They were constructed by Adunai, Ogun

and Oya and made entirely of amber bark. In the corners of the
sanctuary were burning coco palm trees. The flame never singed the
trees but kept the temple lit during their gatherings. Sounds of joy
filled the air as light winds swept across the eve of the day.

Adunai: We give thanks to the Creators for peace and love. They have
given us a chance to reign, so we honor them… always.

Orisha: Honor and order to the Creators! May they never rest and
forever reign!

As the heirs and the Orisha gathered around to eat and give thanks,
they shared their daily lessons and experiences. Laughter and joy
surrounded the night until the indigo moon was at its fullest.

Adunai: You all are my joy. But as Inaru and I left our Creators in
search of more, we were blessed in abundance. Praises to my Lords!
The time has come for you to be blessed beyond measure. It is time to
reach out to the Creators for an introduction.

The Elohii were anxious yet excited. Although they knew of the
Creators and gave thanks to them daily, they had never met them.
Adunai and Inaru embraced one another, placing their crowns to each
other, extending their love to the All. Giza had patiently waited for
centuries to hear from his children and the time had finally arrived.

66

"Can you sense their aura", Giza says excitedly… "they have finally called for us"!

Pisim: Then its best we do not wait any longer.

Giza, Pisim and Anh Sang evaporated unto ElohI and appeared before their descendants.

Okotadi received the will but did not move. He ignored the feeling and continued in his loneliness. When the All appeared, the heirs, Orisha and the Elohii bowed in honor of their presence. The Creators were pleased with how well the heirs maintained their balance throughout the years.

Adunai: My lords, we have honored you since the day we arrived in this quadrant of the multiverse. To have arrived in a world similarly to our lands of Origen, was one of the greatest blessings you have bestowed upon us. We have built temples in your glory and made sure our progeny honor you.

Inaru: Mother, Father…thank you! We have become more and have experienced growth, love, and order. For this we have and will always give you praise.

Elohii: Honor and order to the Creators! May you never rest and forever reign!

The Creators were overwhelmed with joy. Excellence swept throughout all of ElohI. Giza exerted his energy into the grounds of the planet placing more gold essence, diamonds, and jade within her form for longevity.

Giza: May you all continue to thrive and forever reign

Pisim: You all have done beautifully. What have you named the planet?

Adunai: ElohI and our children are the Elohii.

Pisim: The energy upon her is well.

Cocijo and Selu stood in front of the goddess in amazement. Pisim bowed before her descendants, for she was honored to meet them as well.

Giza: Please… allow us to familiarize ourselves.

Inaru: Where is uncle?

The Creators look amongst themselves then unveiled the matters of Okotadi.

Giza: Brother… has fallen ill to the chaos. When you fled, he had become maddened with finding a cure, but his distance along with the harsh environment upon Origen has completely taken him.

Inaru: Could you All not restore his peace?

Giza: He wishes to not be near us. The imbalance within keeps him from us. The domain where we now reside, can only sustain balance and it pains him to be nearby.

Adunai: You must try until he is whole father. Do not allow the chaos to triumph. Not ever!

Giza: You speak with wisdom, a true king. After our visit, we will continue with his restoration.

The Elohii introduced their lands and themselves to the Creators. The Creators were impressed with the new types. Although, the Elohii of Okotadi, were happy to meet the Creators, they were slightly disappointed that they could not meet their God of likeness. The Creators visited upon the lands until the ending of the century, which marked the complete cycle for the heirs. As the time has come for the Creators to leave and attend to Okotadi's restoration, Adunai and Inaru shared some important news with the Elohii.

Inaru: By the rise of the first sun, Adunai and I will become as the Creators. We will have completely matured as you all have. Once the sun rises, we will no longer sit upon ElohI. We will go home to our realm of Origen.

Adunai: We will exist in perfection with the Creators.

Ogun: Will you no longer guide us? Who will rule?

Inaru: We will always be available to you. You only need commune through your auras and the ofrendas in the main sanctuary if need be. We have taught you all that is needed to live in peace. You all have eternal potential, equals and lands to rule upon. We and your Creators of likeness will always be here for you. But the time has come for you all to become more. You all are matured and may increase your kind, but you must maintain the order. Chaos is the absence of peace and will unbalance the planet along with all that she births if it were given the opportunity.

Adunai: We have taught you well. We give you dominion over ElohI. Be pleased.

The heirs and Creators blew happiness upon the crowns of the Orisha and their Elohii as they bowed and gave thanks. Once the rose moon set, the Elohii then returned to their dwellings for rest. As the first sun arose the Creators were gone and the Elohii left behind to live in order.

Once the Creators ascended to the All's heaven, Adunai and Inaru accompanied them. Giza, Pisim and Anh Sang placed their energy around the heirs and balanced them with limitlessness. Although they were unable to create cosmic matter; their existing potential was heightened. Adunai's ability to manipulate lands expanded to include any environment, any terrain throughout the omni verse. He could also sense the auras of his children as well as all other beings across the existences. Inaru could control the emotional state of the omni verse and the weather of all the planets. They both were now the gods over all the realms within the omni verse and the new order was made evident to all organisms of their king god Adunai and queen god Inaru.

8. Harmony

Okotadi received the word of Adunai and Inaru's promotion to perfection as the sonic message spread throughout existences. As the vibe penetrated his ears, the news pleased him, for he remembers loving the heirs. Okotadi took an overwhelming liking to the news. Parts of him began to regenerate. Okotadi took a deep breath. Then he took another and another. As each breath passed, he was reminded of what love from the heirs felt like. He remembered the sound of their voices, their laughter. A moment from his past opened in front his eyes. Okotadi recalled a memory of him Adunai and Inaru from when they were younger and could not perfectly balance the aquatic elements. Okotadi laughed, as he witnessed the heir's weird faces and sounds as they concentrated on balancing water. The energy around his memories surrounded him so deeply that he laughed loudly to himself. Tears fell from his eyes and upon the ground. As Okotadi wiped his eyes, he glanced down and picked a rainbow rose that grew from his tears. Okotadi plucked the rose and smiled joyfully at it and thought how Inaru would love this flora. He could now sense how both Adunai and Inaru made him truly feel. Okotadi lingered with the realities a while longer and upon a final breath Okotadi's pity and depression lifted as his frequency began to harmonize. He knew that it would be nice to visit and honor them with his goodness and gifts.

Just then, angered thoughts attempted to turn his decision, "remember, the look on Giza's face, Adunai and Inaru may both receive you with the same temperament." Okotadi shook the thoughts off, composed himself and continued with his natural intent. As he calmed himself with the thoughts of reuniting with the heirs, his demeanor and body slowly changed to his original form. He was no longer horrid but pleasant to the eye as originally designed. His marbled form regained shape, giving him the statuesque appearance, he was designed with. As parts of his form healed, he was left with a few cracks, but not so much as to distinguish him from being as whole as he could possibly become. The love within him outweighed the pain. Okotadi approached the All's heaven with hesitation, for the last time he visited, the perfection's light burned his form as its sound pierced through his mind. As he reached the edge of the realm, he took a deep breath and entered, but to his surprise he had not been harmed. Anh Sang sensed Okotadi's presence and greeted him with gratification.

Anh Sang: I have been awaiting your arrival my love. You feel well.

Okotadi: I have received the word. I would like to see them as it's been quite some time.

Anh Sang: Yes, it has. Come everyone will be pleased!

When Okotadi entered Giza's realm, he was received better than he had expected. Giza placed his hands upon Okotadi's shoulders, looked deeply upon his face...

Giza: I have been patiently awaiting your return brother. Are you better? You feel it. We have much to do and I would love a match.

Okotadi: I received the word and it eased me from my loathing. I have not known joy for what seems to be an eternity. I am not sure that I am healed, but I love the heirs greatly and wish to see them in their perfected essence.

Giza: Whatever is needed for you to be whole Tadi, simply ask. Come they will be pleased. I am joyed to see you, my brother! We must have a match.

Okotadi imagined the sneers and looks of rejection would be upon their faces, but to his surprise, he was greeted with open arms and not the slightest judgement.

Pisim: Okotadi...you seem well

Okotadi: I am honored to be here, standing amongst all of you.

Inaru: Uncle...

Okotadi: My goddess! How lovely you have grown. It brings me such joy to be in the presence of you and your equal

Okotadi held onto the heirs tightly. Then handed Inaru the rainbow rose that grew from his tears of joy. He then placed his hand upon Adunai's shoulder as he looked at him with joy and honor.

Adunai: My lord… I have missed you

Okotadi: My god… you are strong, like your father. And what is this

Adunai: …uncle, it is a beard

Okotadi: Haha! It suits you… My, how you both have grown. And now… Gods of Excellence! I just recalled moments of you as young forms learning to manipulate elements. It is your love that restored me, and I am forever grateful.

As the All were together laughing and enjoying themselves, it seems as if they had forgotten about the chaos and the destruction of Origen. The harmony within Okotadi restored as the misery inside him slowly began to fade. As time passed Okotadi was content being around his family. Adunai and Inaru shared stories of their children, the Elohii.

Adunai: This has been wonderful. The realms and the omni verses are at peace. The chaos is still eonic lifetimes away from ElohI and our reality is harmonized. It is time that we visit the land.

He looks over at Okotadi with joy…. "All of us."

Giza: Yes, this is wonderful. Inaru announce us.

Inaru synchs into the auras of the Orisha Oya and Hiyori-Li, to inform them of their next visit. As the Orishas receive this message they informed the other Elohii. Once the arrangements were set, the Elder Elohii reached out to the All and awaited their arrival. As the All descend onto ElohI, the people greet them with praise, "Honor and order to the Creators"! Calyx and Rhea were ecstatic, for they were to finally meet their Creator of likeness. He was amazed at how they resembled him in form and potential. They took Okotadi to their land and showed him the temples and statues dedicated to his greatness. This pleased him very much. However, he was extremely impressed with charted elements collected from the planet and the organized classification. "Did you think of this on your own?" Rhea replied, "Calyx and I with the help of Hiyori-Li." He was most impressed as he examined the chart. After visiting with his Orishas of likeness, they all gathered in the main sanctuary to feast and greet one another. Since the departure of the Creators, the Elohii expanded their progeny. Inaru and Adunai, were greeted by the Orisha, and introduced to the new heirs of ElohI. Each of the Orishas birthed children, but they were not in pairs like their parents. The children brought about a new cycle of time. Adunai and Inaru sought to learn about the new heirs and the changes upon ElohI.

Adunai: We have only been gone for a few centuries, and you already have been fruitful (jokingly)

Ogun: This is true father, but they are birthed in order and love as you have birthed us.

Hiyori- Li: The children have shortened the days and nights. Their cycle is younger and requires more attention. Their potential is different.

Adunai: How so?

Kuei-Shen pointed to his sons to come forward. As they approached, they were asked to demonstrate their potential. The sons of the Kuei-Shen and Hiyori-Li stood in front of the All and commenced singing. The purest most serene sounds echoed from their mouths.

Hiyori-Li: Neither of us recognize such a language.

Okotadi and Anh Sang stood over the males and placed symbols to their sound waves. Blessed they were with the language of music.

As they continued singing the waves of tunes collided into various elements; trees, rocks, water, and these surfaces carried the tunes out longer. The pulsating rhythms encouraged Cocijo and Selu to move and sway to it as well as their children. They began to twirl and bounce which made the environment shift into bliss. The heirs of Ogun and Oya were quite fond of the sounds and carried the beats to the water beasts, giving them the language of music as well. Pisim stood over the female types and blessed them with the language of the waters. Allowing them to not only thrive in its environment but manipulate its emotional state as well. The Creators were impressed with the potential of all the Elohii. They bestowed various gifts upon their descendants and the planet. The order made Giza content. He saw all that the Creators made, was good.

After a century upon ElohI, the All decided to leave and return to their realm. They shared and taught the Elohii much during their visit and was there to witness the birth and growth of their kind. However, it was the Elohii who also taught the All much about their kind and the different types of goodness that existed. As the evening sun set, Giza and Okotadi laid upon the fields and played a game...

Okotadi: I don't know why you insist, you never prevail against me.

Giza: I simply enjoy the challenge, even if defeated...

Okotadi: If defeated? (he chuckles)

Giza: I have been waiting for the moment to discuss an issue with you

Okotadi: Anything...

Giza: The chaos? I see it continues to grow and move through space. Are you close to a solution?

Okotadi: I wish to not speak about it while on their world. I fear becoming ill and releasing any toxins, while in the presence of such peace and beauty. But there is a solution, and I will need your assistance. Checkmate brother! Once again

Giza: As you wish.

After the final sun had set, the Elohii honored the All with a feast and a routine of their talents. Music, dance, food, and friendly demonstrations to appease the All and as the first sun arose, they were gone, leaving the Elohii in harmony.

9. Return

Anh Sang and Pisim could not help but remain content, as they spoke amongst themselves. They experienced the births and maturing of the new Elohii generations.

Pisim: Oh Anh! The Elohii are magnificent! The younglings are beautiful and so full of joy and intellect.

Anh Sang: I find them compelling. Their composition is amazing. Have you noticed the seasonal patterns and their sleep patterns?

Pisim: I enjoy that you enjoy their love my sister. I was too distracted with heir cuteness and skills that I had not calculated patterns.

Anh Sang: Don't patronize me Pisim… I'm simply stating that their nocturnal cycle in conjunction with the division of the day, is… as you would say… adorable.

Pisim: Totally, Anh

Inaru and Adunai were pleased with their children and impressed that they have continually maintained the order and balance upon the planet. Giza and Okotadi, had not spoken about the chaos since it had been mentioned on ElohI, but Okotadi knew the time had arrived to put the madness to an end. He gathered the All to discuss, his solution…

Okotadi: A word…All. I have enjoyed being at peace with you and with the Elohii. I must admit that I feared coming to you. Brother, you once told me forgiveness I will always have. Now the time has come where we combine our strengths and put an end to the chaos. Although ElohI's function has deviated, its current existence is of far better use, and I will not see such beauty harmed.

Inaru: Function?

Okotadi: When I unknowingly created the chaos, our arrangement was to create a new mother planet and unleash the imbalance upon her. However, you made it your sanctuary and for this I am glad. She was too glorious for destruction.

Adunai: We assumed that universe was made for Inaru and I. So, once we matured, we could exist? Was this not the intent?

Okotadi: It was not. We had no knowledge of your abilities nor necessities. We wanted to be rid of the chaos, so it would not affect either of you.

Inaru: Although the intent was not in favor of our reign, I am pleased that she was part our destiny.

Okotadi: As am I, your grace. When upon Origen, I noticed the frozen gems on the mountain tops contain the possibility longer than any other structure. I say we build one of massive body to engulf the chaos.

Giza: Where will we place the gem once it holds the chaos captive?

Okotadi: I have not balanced this equation. I cannot be whole, nor rationalize calmly while it exists. The insanity within me has been lulled but, I am not certain for how long. The peace that I feel when around you All make it easier for me to quiet the madness, but I understand that the chaos must be destroyed.

Anh Sang: Before we conclude with this decision. I would like to investigate the planet and the corruption. I would like to make certain of a sound outcome.

Okotadi: Then I shall accompany you

Anh Sang: Your assistance is appreciated but denied. You must remain here in peace. Inaru and I will do the investigation. We will let you know of our findings.

Giza: Agreed. We will not have you falling into despair.

Inaru: No worries uncle, once we have gathered the necessary intel, we will work together in the balancing of your equation.

Okotadi felt a sense of relief that they were all in aid of his restoration. Anh Sang and Inaru left for the planet, Adunai accompanied them as well. Upon entrance to Origen, Adunai fell down to the ground. The color in his form fatigued. The very heart of him ached as he cried out to his mother. As he caressed the ground, he could not hear her but could feel her pulse slowly beating. The stench decayed and withered the grass and hardened the soils. Adunai pounded upon the land and dug his hands deeper. He called out to Origen, but she was very weak and could not answer him. Inaru's eyes swelled with tears as she could sense the planet's anguish. The distress and emptiness of the land removed the joy from her. The trees were broken and scorched. The air was toxic and dry. Many of the animals had vanished. The animals that remained were not as remembered. Their exteriors were dried and cracked. They walked about on the palms of their feet as if to almost escape the heated surfaces. They too were maddened, feeding on one another as well as scavenging on the decayed carcasses.

Anh Sang: Reserve your strength. The chaos will attempt to feed of you. Let us collect what knowledge we can that we may restore her. She is extremely ill, but there is still hope.

Adunai: We will save you mother!

As they roamed the land for answers, Inaru noticed the gems were no longer whole. As she closely examined them, the chaos had peered through by creating small craters for escape.

Inaru: Uncle is mistaken, the gems will not contain the chaos... it has managed to seep through.

Anh Sang: I noticed this... look here. The containment within a gem does more harm than he'd expected. Granted the gems hydrogenated composition and hardened surface along with the crystal's refracting capabilities, this option poisoned the intentions rather than contained them. Due to its transparent multi faced exterior, various distorted images are reflected into the environment. He had been creating more chaos. Therefore, the lands are diminishing rapidly.

I wonder...Okotadi should have been able to calculate these actions.

Inaru: What are you saying?

Anh Sang: Perhaps...If the chaos has intelligence and wants to breed destruction then Okotadi is being made to believe the crystal is the only way. His own intelligence would have accounted for the chemical reactions of this, I am sure of it. Do not say a word to him. Let us find an alternate approach.

Adunai: If the chaos is intelligent then, it has been controlling uncle.

Inaru: But to what degree?

Anh Sang: Do not worry, his peace has been stable. Bringing Okotadi here to provide a result of failure may trigger him. We will find a way. For now, we let him know that we are working on a solution to his equation. We will meet here in a few days' time. Ascend, I want to see if there are any clues in his realm.

Adunai: I will not leave you here. We ascend together or not at all.

Anh Sang: As you wish

Upon entering Okotadi's realm, they noticed layers and layers of stars containing maddened possibilities. Not the slightest glimmer of joy existed anymore. The once luminous skies were dark and dreary.

Inaru: Uncle has succumbed to the darkness...there is no hope here! And what of all this? There is enough here to destroy mother and her universe!

Adunai: He has not been honest with us.

Anh Sang: No, he has not! The destruction is using your uncle's intelligence. His insanity seems to have dark logic of some sort. Neither of us, have knowledge of this unstable energy. We will not know how to rid of it. I must speak to it

Inaru: No! It could get hold of you! We do not need your intelligence and potential compromised and maddened! Without you we will never figure out a solution to stop it!

Adunai: Inaru is correct. We will find a way that does not affect anyone else. First uncle, now Origen… the casualties have been plenty.

Anh Sang: I will, reason with him. It is the only way to understand what we are working against. Furthermore, I am not seeking your approval rather your assistance!

Adunai and Inaru: Yes, my lord!

As they travel back, Okotadi greets them anxiously

Okotadi: What have you learned? Do you believe the gems will work?

Inaru: There is so much destruction upon mother. We are taking our time to find a solution to your equation. We believe the crystals could work, but Anh Sang suggests we do more research, that we may account for all outcomes.

Okotadi: Yes. Is there anything that I can do?

Anh Sang: Yes. But we will wait a few days' time to meet upon Origen. I would like for you to assist with the hypothesis.

Okotadi: Yes, anything. I want to rid of this chaos and restore their mother.

In the days to come Anh Sang visited the mother planet to find a solution. She worked diligently alongside versions of herself to maximize efficiency. They collected the samples, tested theories, and adjusted methods. Anh Sang was in Okotadi's realm educating herself on the possibilities trapped within. As she magnifies an asteri before her, closely examining the contents…

Anh Sang: It seems to be ravenous... and forcing themselves through the barrier of the asteri...fascinating!

Meanwhile in Giza's realm, Okotadi grew impatient and restless. He gained the urge to lend a hand. He believed that he had been at peace enough to assist. Although everyone, including Okotadi agreed it was best he does not visit Origen; Okotadi grew anxious and evaporated onto the planet. As Okotadi looked around he began to feel horrible. He could not believe the amount of mayhem he caused. He looked upon the mountain tops and saw the crystals had dissolved into volcanic boulders. He assumed the gems would hold the chaos, but it seems that he did not calculate the crystal's chemistry. This was odd, and such a rudimentary mistake on his behalf. As he entered his realm, he finds Anh Sang looking through the stars. He was in awe at the pile of impurities he had released.

Okotadi: (stammering) I...I... I do not.... uh understand... it is as if I am seeing for the first time, the damage. Damage, that I have created (sadly)

Anh Sang: There is enough destruction to dismantle time and existences and you cannot recall how this came to be...

Okotadi: I do not...

Anh Sang: I have acquired my own calculation. The chaos uses your intelligence against you. It has been deceiving you. Making you believe the crystal is the best approach. However, the refractory compound of the crystals…

Okotadi: (exhales sorrowfully) …distort and reflect the images from within…

As Okotadi and Anh Sang worked diligently on finding a solution, the voice buried deep within Okotadi began to disturb him, "she wants your knowledge, your power…she always has". He tried to ignore it and continued working. After some time, the voice in his head blurred his sight.

Okotadi: (Frustratedly) Come! Let us take a moment to understand what we have so far.

Anh Sang sensed his aura had adjusted but remained as if she had not noticed.

Anh Sang: We cannot stop until we have solved it.

Okotadi: Yes Anhy, and I love your diligence…but I am feeling odd and need a moment to breathe.

Anh Sang: Yes, of course.

As they both stepped out of Okotadi's realm, they sat upon the discs of a neighboring planet to reflect. Anh Sang sent one of her versions to witness from a safe distance. They sat in peace gazing at the magnificence before them. They sat and watched a group of stars achieve solar dynamic. The stars were not organic, yet their auto-intelligent design was a wonder to witness. The stars would glow into existence, orbit one another, produce more stars, and then bursts into atomic particles, that spread around the omniverse providing it with light. As they watched the newly made energy shoot around and beyond space, Okotadi felt a sense of hopelessness come over him. Before he could begin speaking Anh Sang interrupted...

Anh Sang: The moment we became into existence, I could sense your potential. I could feel its pull to me and me to it. You have the most intoxicating aura I have ever known. Your intelligence attracts me. Your accuracy intrigues me. Your logic, the passion I feel is...immeasurable! Your capabilities to create forces with such ease is truly admirable. But you must always maintain your peace. The same desire within you to destroy is just as powerful. If it takes control, it will leave you empty. And once completely taken... (Anh Sang shed tears at the mere thought of such a thing), you will no longer exist, and I will cease to endure. I love you infinitely Tadi!

Okotadi: The chaos cannot destroy what we have made.

Anh Sang: Then do not allow it!

Anh Sang placed her happiness upon his crown. As they returned to Okotadi's realm, he was hopeful, yet frightened to look within the stars. He had not wanted to remind himself of what he could and had become. As Anh Sang sorted through the possibilities, she came across one so vile that it slipped from her hands and shattered upon the scorched surface, immediately releasing vapors from within. Anh Sang turned to Okotadi instantly with the intent to evaporate before it affected him, but the lunacy in his eyes stared directly at her the exact moment of approach.

Anh Sang: My equal...restore your peace

As she uttered these words a tear slowly fell from the corner of her eye, for Okotadi's gemmed claws drove through Anh Sang's celestial form the moment she approached him. Agony and death released into her. She looked deeply into his face as the hate coiled around her harmony, slowly dismantling her core. Anh Sang smiled peacefully at Okotadi, shut her eyes then disbursed into sonic energy. Okotadi gathered her notes in his palms, then blew them throughout the neighboring realms. Once Okotadi destroyed Anh Sang his celestial form began to pain him. His skin singed then peeled off and turned to ash as it hit the ground beneath him. Okotadi yelled, the molting of his skin and manic transformation was excruciating. Okotadi fell to the grounds, gasping intensely for a breath. His golden essence began to pour from his eyes, nose, ears, and mouth. As Okotadi seized form trembled across his realm, his once sky filled form had become corrupted flesh. His veins ran red essence as his newly transparent

90

skin blistered. Okotadi had become naked. After his conversion, Okotadi arose, saw his reflection, and slowly began to inspect himself. The imbalance stared back at Okotadi, then grinned with disdain. Anh Sang's version looked upon them as instructed but did not interfere out of obedience. She sent the vision for the All to witness then faded out of existence. The unbalancing of the All had emerged.

10. Submit

Pisim gasped deeply. Her form became asphyxiated and began to diminish in vibrancy. She was immediately weakened by the destruction of Anh Sang. While Pisim convulsed and throttled upon grounds, Giza, Adunai and Inaru watched the reality Anh Sang's version had released unto them before disbursing. They were all traumatized with excruciating heartache. Adunai had become so enraged, so vexed that without hesitation he burst from the All's heaven... Giza and Inaru followed, but only to divert Adunai.

Giza: Noooo! Adunai, Noo! Look at me... Son, LOOK...AT...ME!

Giza's heart was hurt for the death of Anh Sang and the loss of his brother, but he could not allow his strength to fall into despair. Giza intercepted Adunai, becoming a large wall to block his path. But Adunai, so full of rage and pain, permeated through Giza's guard upon contact. Giza intercepted Adunai a few more times, becoming shields, then earthen containers and iron laced orbs, to engage Adunai and slow his efforts to approach Okotadi. Giza struggled with grasping Adunai's attention. Giza could not allow Adunai to succumb to Okotadi's vices. "Look at me son! Look! It ...will... consume you! This is what the imbalance wants! To divide and conquer us... listen to me... let us return!"

Inaru fused with Giza, attempting to regulate Adunai's rage. She extended her aura around the orb Giza used to capture Adunai. Utilizing her root chakra, Inaru slowly began to compel Adunai, securing his emotions and making him feel more like himself, "My Equal... please, father is correct. Please, let us return. We will find a way to deal with the imbalance and make it pay for all it has taken!"

Adunai: He... He... Uncle...aaaaaaahhhhhhh!!!!!

Adunai's pain shot through the barriers of the universes so much, that it disrupted the atmosphere upon ElohI. His rage and sorrow swept upon the planet for many, many days, bringing forth earthquakes and rainstorms in the likes of which the Elohii have never seen. As Adunai's fury faded Giza was finally able to embrace his son. Giza cautiously placed Adunai within his loving and powerful source, so Adunai's peace would not break, but remain whole. As they returned to the temples above Origen, they found Pisim weakened. She was greatly affected by the death of her sister. Inaru laid beside her mother, attempting to bring her comfort. Giza and Adunai placed their focus upon Origen. They watched as Okotadi befell. Okotadi, turned looking upward and pointing in the All's direction as he slowly and deliberately placed algorithms around the planet. He then fled in ElohI's direction placing algorithms to deny the All access to both Origen and ElohI.

Adunai: No! He cannot have my children!

Giza: We will find a way to counter

The All tried meticulously to find a catalyst to Okotadi's equations, but had fallen short of a stable product, every time. Inaru aided in balancing outcomes, but without Anh Sang's intellect, their attempts rendered useless. Pisim fluttered in an out of consciousness, until the moment she fell so deep within herself. Pisim stood, touched her form, for it was no longer fevered. She looked around the unfamiliar realm, until…

Pisim: Anhy! O my sister! What… how… how are you here? Where is here?

Anh Sang: I removed a sliver of my form and informed her to remain, that she could warn you All of Okotadi. I had been examining him since our beginning. After my delta version reflected my death to you All, she began to fade from existence as I already had, but the Am collected her, thus bringing my consciousness here. We are within her essence.

Pisim: We…are…within Am?

Light and sound particles appeared before Pisim and Anh Sang. Crystalized amber cells created a form unlike Pisim had ever witnessed. The Am was not matter like the goddess, but the original source of energy. She shimmered and emitted frequency. Her appearance was that of the spectrum of light which changed in color as she spoke...

Am: You both are so beautiful. So graceful. So loving. I have been waiting for a moment such as this, but it cannot take place while you physically exist. As you both were created from my essence to my essence you shall return.

Pisim: I no longer exist?

Am: Your form is very weak. But you are deep within the caverns of your consciousness. So much so, that you are in your past, which is slightly after my beginning. That is where I exist and where we are now, but I will send you back to deliver my decrees.

Anh Sang: Okotadi is enraged, by a force unlike any other.

Am: Infinitus, your father. He is the absence of light and sound. Before we encountered, I had not known of any other existence. I had only known my light, my harmony. I had come to realize through your being, what lies in the dark and silent. There is a blistering emptiness. I now understand that his and my combining created you All. For this I am joyed, but ever since then I dwell deep within you, as he does within my kings. His energy as you have witnessed in Okotadi is darkened and aiming to consume the light and sound. This cannot happen, for I will cease to exist as well as the All that you have become. He and I must be restored to our Origen of existence.

Pisim: But how my Am? We have never encountered such a force and he has almost destroyed us.

Am: You must love Okotadi to peace. There was a moment when the Infinity and I realized that we were not alone. He had shown me wonders and I he. But after a while, he attempted to silence me. To place me, to keep me within his darkness. We struggled with one another, until...

Anh Sang: ... Until we came into existence.

Am: Precisely. You must make Okotadi remember what it is to be whole. What it is to be loved. It is the Infinite's nature to remain obsolete. Once Okotadi and the Infinity have remembered, you take the opportunity to restore Okotadi's balance. This will suppress them both, not for long, but enough to separate us.

Pisim: What will you have me do?

Am: You must send Inaru and Adunai through time. They must be birthed as the people yet reign supreme among them. They must achieve balance over the lifetimes where Okotadi is master. They must spread my decrees of light and harmony amongst all of the Elohii. They must always be reminded to rise and reinforce harmony during moments of chaos. There will be many battles, many lives lost, but Giza, once merged with you, Anh and myself can convert them into sacrifices. There is no greater love than to die for those you love. These sacrifices will also aid in weakening the many spells Okotadi has placed over humanity. Once Okotadi is fully weakened Giza will need to restore his peace and balance his brother. Their balance will restore Anh Sang to full existence. Then it will be up to you All, to return Infinitus and myself to our original states. Once you have paralleled with the beginning, we will continue to our individual existences.

Anh Sang: You mean return to the beginning? Before any of us?

Am: Return prior to the beginning. It is the only way to end the suffering. He and I cannot be combined. For he will not stop until he has brought about complete absence.

Pisim: Then Giza and I shall send the young gods through time along with the decrees.

Pisim extended her palms towards the Am as her lyrical decree became scripted all over Pisim's form… *"Blessed are those aflame in the purity of my light. Humble are those that take refuge in my sound. May my Orders of existence forever be engraved into the essence of the righteous. Protected are they by the supreme source* of animate life. As first mother I hereby bestow excellence upon the potential of those descendant from High God Adunai, High Goddess Inaru and the harmony of ElohI. I bring forth the Acceptance, the Awareness, and the Awakening to reign upon the purest of Elohii Elders until a time before the beginning has been brought forth. May the energy that sustains you, never rest and forever reign."

Once the Am confirmed the decrees, it resonated within the potential of Anh Sang and Pisim. "This is where we part hermana", Anh embraces Pisim then places an Amethyst quartz within her crown. "It will help sustain your form and our eternal connection."

As the Am, Pisim and Anh Sang departed from one another, Pisim's conscience was sent back to her form. Pisim awakened and stood up instantly, for she knew there was no time to waste in delivering Am's message. As she stood, she noticed Am's language tattooed all over her form and could feel the connection of her ancestry within her crown. Giza, Adunai and Inaru were happy to see Pisim awake…

Pisim: Okotadi must be stopped. He is being driven by our father, Infinitus, the absence of both light and sound. It is his will that compels brother to madness. The Infinite seeks to obliterate the source of any other existence. Okotadi needs to be balanced. Through honest sacrifice and love. This will weaken him.

Inaru: What will you have us do?

Pisim: We must distribute powers across time lived and times yet to come. Decrees that will help launch Inaru and Adunai a winning chance.

Inaru: How much time?

Pisim: Millenia fold… or as many as it takes, but the decrees must be released at the precise moment.

Inaru: The Elohii will all be destroyed if they must wait so long. There must be another way, without condemning them to such suffering. The 2nd millennia is already upon ElohI! And we must wait exponentially longer!

Giza: Your mother and I will protect as many as we can, I give you, my word!

Pisim: Many will continue to perish my love and for this I ache, but Okotadi must be stopped. It is the absence that fuels him. Okotadi designed ElohI with more resources and mass than Origen, so we must wait until the exact moment, to dismantle the chaos from within. Giza and I will send and guide you, but you must remain balanced. If you are not, I don't think we will remain connected. As the age of prophecy emerges for your descendants, they will feel the full effects of the Destruction across lifetimes. You both are divinely paired and thus will always find one another… your potential wills it. Through selfless sacrifice you will begin to weaken him and gain strength. You must tell others and spread the good news. Support and love your fellow man, be their strength. Awaken the Elohii who will have forgotten of their essence over time. They will need you for survival. They will need to be disciplined once again in the ways of the Order. Natural decrees will be put in place as the generations of Elohii populate the planet. The more descendants that believe and live their lives by these decrees will be honored. However, Okotadi with his logic may learn of this. He will analyze the various possibilities and realities in order to secure successful outcomes. But he has no idea about the Am's logic and for this first time will not have knowledge of, nor anticipate Giza's move.

Inaru: How will we know what to do?

Pisim: We will forever be with you. Blessed will be your ancestors and blessed will be your futures. Our love will be sent with you. Your father is making the preparations. Always remember…Darkness cannot drive out darkness, only light can do that. Hate cannot drive out hate, only love can do that.

Giza and Pisim embraced the heirs as their love surrounded them, equipping their essence with powers of compassion, courage, peace, and awareness. Adunai and Inaru bowed before their parents, in respect of their trust and pledged, "Honor and order unto the Creators." Adunai turned towards Inaru and held her near him. He looked pleasantly upon her face and caressed it gently. He then blew happiness upon her crown.

Adunai: May the energy that sustains you, never rest my love.

Inaru: I will always find you Dune. There is no lifetime that will deny our love.

Inaru and Adunai looked deeply upon each other as Giza extracted their essence and placed it within the stillness of time. As many lifetimes as you need. As the heirs were released into eternity Giza, then turned his attention to his equal. He sorrowed to see her in such a desolate state.

Pisim: They will be fine. We are with them

Giza: I am with you

Giza caressed Pisim's nose and upon her cheeks and slowly toward her frontal. Giza savored the moment, for his love was so true of Pisim. He placed his mouth upon her crown, then slowly began to inhale Pisim until she was fully within his aura. Pisim's pure light attached to Giza's vast darkened colored form. It illuminated brightly, taking over Giza's dim physique, then moments later, Pisim's weather essence reflect as the chakras on Giza's form. Linking his masculinity with Am, Pisim and Anh Sang's auras. He had truly become the last of Origen's Creators. Giza manifested and transformed into the first chief god. He split his heavens and the realms of his sisters. He decreed that the essence of his descendants would return unto him as they perished during the lifetimes. Their power would be used to fuel Giza's essence against Okotadi. Giza turned his attention towards ElohI. He focused Pisim's light upon the planet and the people. He extended his palms as Pisim's light was also blasted into time. Giza knew the chaos was no match for its purity and knew the protection would withstand time itself.

Now, Giza waits…

As my mind and my body slowly began to come together, I saw Elegua's face looking at me with that same peaceful smile. He nodded his head as if I had done a good job at something. As I sat in this cave recollecting on the visions shown to me while analyzing the language tatted on my body, I understood that the Origen was part of me; part of my destiny, but still uncertain what that would be. I just witnessed the birth of everything! I had so many questions… but before I could open my mouth to get a word out, Elegua blew his happiness upon my forehead and suddenly I was back in my car. DJ E-Zone was still spinning from the crates as Brandy "I wanna be down" was playing in my background. I sat there in a daze pinching my forearm, which I could feel while staring out of the window and at the moon. She was big, beautiful, golden, and full. I stared at the moon until the giant cloud that shrouded it broke my concentration. By the time I sort of came to, I had been in my car all night long. I didn't even make it to see Ragnarök. As I exited my car at 1:11am, I walked back into the house, locked the door where my sister was awake watching tv in the living room. She asked, "how was the movie?", walking towards my room without even looking in her direction I replied, "I never made it I was in a cave all night", then walked into my room, changed my clothes, laid in the bed, and stared at the ceiling until I fell asleep.

11. Damn

I just could not shake that night. Every day I waited for something magical to happen but then began to feel really foolish when nothing did. I wondered where Elegua went and why was I only visited once if I had something so important to do. Every time I brought up that night my sister kept repeating that I had must of gotten really high before leaving the house. And while there is some truth to that, grapefruit kush is everything, I don't ever get too high, especially if I'm going to be driving. I assured her that I was not. I even managed to take pictures of the bruises on my arm from the repeated pinches.

Leslie: How do you explain these pinches if that night wasn't real.

J: That has nothing to do with nothing

Leslie: I only pinch myself during bad dreams and if I can't feel them then I know I'm dreaming. But I could feel these, I was actually awake. You saw me go to the car…

J: I don't know, it just doesn't make any sense

Leslie: I know! Why would I lie, tho?

J: Maybe you pinched yourself physically, but was dreaming…

Leslie: That's just dumb…

I left the conversation upset. Later that night I sat on the porch reflecting on the vision. As I sat there, I saw a shooting star. While I didn't think anything of it, I saw another shooting start, then another. I stood up as a shower of stars beyond anything I'd ever experienced lit the sky before me. I looked around the neighborhood to see if there was anyone else seeing this shit. I didn't see a neighbor in sight, I poked my head in the door, "aye J come here, quick" … as she stepped onto the porch… "what"? and just that quickly the stars were gone. There wasn't even a trace of their light in the sky. My sister peered at me, and I got upset all over again, slamming the door behind me "aaaahhhh, never mind!!!"

As I paced back in forth in my room I was truly bothered, because something was happening to me, and I didn't know what. I tried Googling my experience, but only found articles about near-death experiences. I took a few deep breaths, lit a candle, sat down in criss cross applesauce, and started meditating…

Leslie: Ok Jehovah. I have been to church and talked to the sister about what happened and got nowhere. I have been in the bible and no leads. Please tell me what is happening. You clearly sent Elegua my way. What does he or you need me to do?

I sat there for so long that I eventually laid on the floor and fell asleep. Once again, I found myself in the shadows of ElohI…

After Adunai and Inaru's ascension, the Orishas continued to live peacefully. They tended to the duties expected of their essence and gathered in the evenings to feast and commune.

Once upon a day, the Elohii of Okotadi, Rhea and Calyx were in the fields collecting foods for the evening gathering, when they noticed that many of the pear berries in the orchard were overly ripened and many had withered upon the grass. As they both noticed these changes, they had also detected that the flora of the outer rim of the garden seemed typical, but the trees towards the center and next to the ponds were darkened and spotted. Even the grass beneath appeared damaged.

Calyx: What do you suppose happened?

Rhea: I assume the lands will experience many changes with the departure of our King-father and Queen-mother.

Calyx: Do you think we will see them again?

Rhea: Perhaps, the Creators have visited us many times and will continue to do so. They will never forsake us.

Calyx: What of our lord, they say he is maddened.

As these words carried into the passing breeze, Okotadi stood from behind the waterfall. No longer horrid and blistered but appeared bright and beautiful.

Calyx: My lord?!

Okotadi: Rhea. Calyx. What joy it is to see you?

Rhea: We were unaware of your arrival.

Okotadi: I have returned, simply to admire the harmony upon this planet. She is unlike any other in the multiverse. But please, continue with your daily duties. I am not here to make a fuss, simply enjoy and learn of ElohI's environment.

Rhea: Your presence is never a distraction, my lord. Honor and Order unto you always.

As these Orisha stood before Okotadi in admiration, Rhea noticed that the steps Okotadi left behind were similar to the scorched markings upon the flora.

Rhea: We were simply gathering for our evening's feast. Will you honor us?

Okotadi: I humbly decline. As mentioned, I will continue to explore, examine, you all enjoy the evening.

Rhea bowed before Okotadi as did Calyx. As they continued with their works, Rhea expressed what she had noticed to Calyx.

Rhea: His heels mark the ground beneath him. The mark is extremely similar to those within the orchard and upon the fruit. His aura did not feel trustworthy as he spoke. I do not believe he is here simply to admire and learn.

Calyx: What could he possibly be here for? He is our lord, he created such a place for us, he may choose to be about the lands, without our permission or guidance.

Rhea: Perhaps? But his presence is the only change between our last gathering and the overly ripened fruits.

As the evening brought forth sweet winds and light rain, the Orishas settled into the sanctuary for dinner and spoke of their day.

Calyx: Did you know? Our lord walks about this planet spreading his greatness.

Ogun: Okotadi is here?... Upon ElohI? I cannot feel his light within our lands. The gods have always made themselves known before an arrival, why would he not allow us to provide him a worthy greeting?

Rhea: There is overly ripened fruit and burnt flora next to the pond from which he ascended.

Hiyori: Anomaly...why did he not, descend? Why did he not come from above, as they always have. If he ascended, where did he come from?

Calyx: Rhea believes he is the reason for these irregularities. Do you think that he is still maddened?

Oya: It could possibly be. One of you must reach out to your Creator and seek counsel. We must know if he is dangerous.

Ogun stood immediately and headed towards the ofrenda; alters for connecting with the Creators directly. These alters were gifts given unto the Elohii by the Creator Pisim as a means of communication and reverence. As he approached Giza's ofrenda to connect, Ogun took a deep breath, illuminated Giza's torch, tambo each bata drum and prepared his mind for the connection. However, Ogun's concentration was broken the moment Okotadi walked into the sanctuary unannounced.

Okotadi: The winds here are sweet, as were the days of Origen (inhales deeply).

Hiyori: My Lord, please enter. This is such an honor.

Okotadi: I am simply here to admire, examine, learn. The beauty of this planetess, is so enchanting.

Ogun: We bless the Mother. She keeps us and we her.

Rhea: ...have you noticed markings near the orchard and pond?

Okotadi: Markings? No, why I cannot say that I have. Are the Oaks weakening, by any chance?

Rhea: I've noticed these changes, just recently and thought you may know something of it.

Okotadi: I'm sorry my dear. However, we can explore its finding in the wake of the first sun.

Calyx: Sounds great my Lord, now come join us and feast.

As the first sun approached Rhea and Calyx headed out to practice their potential for the day. As they neared the orchard, Calyx saw that the scorched marks were removed and the fruit in bloom once more.

Rhea: Oh good, the markings are gone.

Calyx: Odd, they were here before and now they have disappeared, after informing Okotadi about it.

Rhea: Whatever was marking it, has gone

Okotadi: Not gone, perceived differently.

Okotadi removed their present reality, grabbed Rhea and placed her closely in front of him.

Calyx: What are you doing? Where are we?

Okotadi: As you rested, I placed you both upon Origen.

Calyx: Why?

Okotadi: You all were made for me, made in my image, and therefore bear the potential for more. The time has come for you to know me, to reason with my logic.

Okotadi placed Rhea in a trance, as he turned Calyx to a statue.
Okotadi placed Rhea into the grounds of Origen for three days. On
the fourth day during the first sun Rhea rose out of the ground. As she
looked around, Rhea became frightened. "Okotadi!", she shouted and
immediately Okotadi approached her; no longer beautiful, but horrid
to the eyes. His aura was dim. His feet were sharp with foul claws.
His eyes piercing and focused like an eaglen. As Okotadi encircled
Rhea, a foul stench perfumed from his form, as he stopped in front of
her admiring her type. He constricted her arms to her body and set
her gaze upon his face. As he opened his mouth, his viperid tongue
slithered outward and placed his forked tongue near Rhea's lips. Rhea
was bewildered but could not retreat, for she was completely
paralyzed, yet aware. Okotadi's spell was extremely powerful. As she
turned her eyes to look away, Okotadi placed both of his hands to
Rhea's face, then the viper slowly entered her mouth and made its
way to her heart, then struck Rhea's life force with its poisoned fangs.
The pain surged through Rhea's form. The viper struck again and
again and again and again and again! Rhea's light poured out from
her eyes, nose and through her fingertips, evaporating the moment it
touched the ground. The light within her form began to dim until all
of her essence was fully drained. As the viper exited Rhea's body, it
slithered back into Okotadi's mouth, then he replaced his will within
her potential and darkened her aura. He rubbed his decrepit form

upon Rhea and engulfed her within his toxicity. Once complete Okotadi placed her in the ground once more and upon the fourth day she had risen. As Rhea shed the last layer of terrain from her form, Calyx was simultaneously released from his spell. As Rhea emerged Calyx was overjoyed.

Calyx: I have been waiting for days my love. What has he done to you?

Rhea: Nothing, he placed me in the ground to rest, the journey here weakened me.

Calyx: I can feel it as well, but I can no longer sense your light. Are you certain that he hasn't done anything to you?

Okotadi: I see you have risen. Have you shared your potential with your equal Rhea? I need you both to stand by me

Calyx: I am not sure what you are up to, but we will not stand with the imbalance.

Okotadi: But you will

After Okotadi whispered in Rhea's ear, he evaporated, and she then turned to Calyx. The scene around them changed back to the orchard from ElohI.

Calyx: Rhea my love, Okotadi is a trickster!

Rhea: He has given me knowledge, he has shown me that he is not all bad, but ahead of his reasoning and that the other sources refused to acknowledge his truths. Therefore, he has shared with me, the truth and now I must teach you, my king.

Calyx: Rhea, he is a deceiver, he is not well

Rhea stood before Calyx. Her form began to pulsate sound waves. Her body following the soft binaural tune. Rhea spread her energy around Calyx. Once his form became relaxed, Rhea placed her kiss upon him. Venom seeped from her lips and into Calyx's body. The venom pierced through his skin and spread through his form. The venom stung Calyx momentarily, then what should have been agony became pure sensation for Calyx. He attempted to fight through it, but the toxicity became pleasurable. Once the venom flowed through his essence Calyx dominated Rhea as they both created upon the lands of Origen. Hail fell from the skies, while cyclones spun out of control demolishing all in its path. Obstruction weathered upon Origen for nine days, until equaled beings emerged from out the volcanos. Lava erupted, spilling down the shaft of the mountains. Semi reptilian and bewitched figures crawled out of molten pods. The female forms emerged first. **Mentira** and **Psyche,** titans and sisters born from the repurposed Orisha Rhea and Calyx and birthed of the corrupted atmosphere of Origen. They were both slender in stature and covered in scales like serpents. Mentira had spikes all over her head and daggered claws. She could imitate others, vanish, and create illusions. Psyche's form was that of a poisonous viper. She had a forked tongue and even spoke with a hiss. She could secrete venom as well as shapeshift. The males arrived moments later in larger molten pods. **Malice** and **Atticus** titans and brothers born from the repurposed Orisha Rhea and Calyx and birthed of the corrupted atmosphere of Origen. Malice was Mentira's equal, he was enormous semi reptilian yet favored his father. He had four bolstering arms. Atticus was Psyche's equal. He was pleasant to the eye just as Okotadi had been before his fall, and was fixated with casting spells, poison making and aiding his Lord Okotadi. Together they were known as the **Destruction**. Their existence brought forth a new cycle of devastation to Origen which strengthened Okotadi. Rhea and Calyx immediately commanded the obedience of their anti-Orisha heirs, demanding they populate an army. As the decades passed upon Origen, the Destruction produced children of their own; **Eliites**. These descendants were cainabels; devourers of Elohii and born to serve Okotadi in the ways of Chaos.

12. Battle of the First

As the years passed on, the disappearance of Calyx and Rhea had not become forgotten. Their progeny Ambrosia, Alpha and Libra continued to display potential, but frequently found themselves hoping and praying for the return of their king father and queen mother. Ogun and the other Orishas spread the workload of the lands equally, which helped the heirs of the misplaced lords maintain Calyx and Rhea's Gardens. In the years to come the Elohii gathered every night within the sanctuary. The desperate, yet patient Elohii lit the ofrendas of the Creators every night since Okotadi's appearance and disappearance of Calyx and Rhea. Seven suns had ripened and yet there was still no sign of them. Although they continued to exercise their potential and maintain the Order upon the planet, the Elohii knew Okotadi was the cause of the Creator's explicit silence.

Selu: Seven suns! And not one word!

Cocijo: We must not lose faith… it is evident that they must be occupied. Continue to have patience.

Selu: …and what about Ambrosia, Alpha, and Libra? They are strong but their auras are filled with worry about their parents.

Cocijo: If… their parents are alive, I truly doubt that they continue to serve the Order. We are here for them now.

The following day as Orisha Hiyori-Li and the Elohii progeny concluded their work in the Spring meadows beyond the Templo Elohii, they all found themselves intrigued by small sprinkles of light, that flurried down from the skies above. This phenomenon was odd to Hiyori, yet it excited the children. As the glimmer fell upon their forms, it dripped off their bodies like water. The Orishas had not experienced such a miracle in many suns. Hiyori and a few of the older progeny gathered the children and headed towards the sanctuary for they knew peculiar times were at hand. Hiyori-Li expedited the progeny, "let's go everyone, quickly." The Orishas placed all the children into the sanctuary, secured its doors, and placed the warrior female types, progeny of Oya and Ogun known as the Dahomey. They were the first line of defense of the main temple. As the sparkling rain poured upon the honey blossom plants, out sprouted gifts. Ogun and Cocijo approached inquisitively...

Cocijo: It appears, to be... weapons?

Ogun looked to the sky and placed his hand upon his forehead in honor of the Creators. Come let us bring these gifts to the storage.

Oya: Weapons (excitedly)! The rainbow blades are definitely mine!

Ogun cheers "Ayabu Nikua!" with his fist over his heart and love in his eyes... for he knew that his queen would unleash her full warrior potential upon any invader with the edge of her blades.

Oya: If a battle is what they seek! (as she flexes a fierce Dambe technique). Come my darlings, the All have provided weapons and gifts for each of us…

As Cocijo and Ogun bring the weapons before the sanctuary, the Dahomey retrieved from the various weapons designed to match their potential.

Yemaya: Yes! Aquamarine daggers… Praises to Giza!

Vocal, the only Elohii without sound searches through the chest, picks up golden mitts outlined in silver, iron, and ivory stones. She tries them on, balls her fists, kisses them both, smiles, then walks off throwing shadow jabs. The others gather around giving thanks and displaying techniques with their weapons.

Alpha: If weapons have rained upon us then this means we are at war and must battle anyone who approaches… even maybe, our lords. I've felt the loss of light between us for many seasons. This is the first time that I admit to it.

Ambrosia: So have I, but fear not… Okotadi will feel our pain and much more. Praises Giza… these iron tipped arrows will definitely do the job! Here Brosia (handing her an Excalibur double bladed sword), this will surely bring victory!

Hiyori-Li: Before Okotadi's madness, they loved you, but now it seems that we have been asked to become defenders of this world and one another. We are your family and I love you girls... have courage. Libra here, these Topaz whips suit you, now chin up and tap into your full essence.

As the Orishas and the Elohii gathered their weapons, they also gathered food, water, supplies and began to secure the lands. Setting up sentry posts. The Orisha would train from the rise of the first sun until the setting of the first moon. They trained as well as stood guards in shifts as to not be surprised by an attack. Two full years had passed as the Elohii prepared and trained. Then upon a day Giza had finally sent a message. Both Adunai and Inaru appeared upon ElohI to help defend the planet and their descendants.

Ogun: Mother!? Father!?

Inaru: We have not abandoned you. Okotadi has created far more trouble than we could have ever known, and we have suffered magnanimously!

Adunai: We do not have much time, for the Destruction are on their way!

Libra: What of our mother and father, your Grace?

Adunai: They are no longer part of the Order…furthermore they have bred the Destruction, and this is why… we are here.

Alpha: Bred the Destruction… what does that mean?

Libra: (frustrated and pissed) It means that we have corrupted siblings, that do not serve the Order and that our queen and king are not familiar to us anymore!

Everyone gathered around to adhere the Gods' message…

Inaru: Giza has sent us to deliver decrees throughout time with an ordinance that will take us to where Okotadi is supreme ruler of both ElohI and her descendants.

Ogun: Will this not be the end of it? Won't we win this battle?

Adunai: I'm afraid not. The true source of light and sound has prophesied, that the battle of Firsts will separate us from our descendants. The Chaos will continue to spread for lifetimes, but…whatever happens… remain… at… peace! Everyone here, remain at peace, trust in Giza, trust in the Order with all your heart but you fight with every element of your potential!!!

Suddenly, A blazing meteor crashed before the sanctuary. The lands trembled upon impact scorching the ground beneath as heat oozed from its crevices. The incinerated shell crumbled upon the ground like ash. As the Orishas and the Elohii assembled for the attack Adunai stood firm before them with Inaru by his side. Out of the shell emerged Mentira and Psyche, female figures of Calyx and Rhea and equal parts of the Destruction.

Adunai: We do not need your presence here… leave!!!

Mentira: Forgive our intrusion my grace, but we are here to meet our sisters. Think of our presence as a union of some sort. Ambrosia, Alpha, and Libra…I am Mentira, this is our lovely sister Psyche. Both mother and father send their love. They thought it would be nice to become… better acquainted (sarcastically).

Alpha: Sister, allow us to skip the formalities… but you, were instructed to leave!

Mentira: Ooh…you sound like you mean it. Psyche, what do you think? Perhaps we should back off.

Psyche: You might be right ssssis (showing off her serpent tongue) … Mal is much better at introductionsss.

Another blazing meteor had fallen from the sky that was twice the size of the meteor that carried the female Destruction to ElohI. Out of the debris stood a giant before them. He was known as Malice, part of the Destruction and Mentira's equal. He stood as tall as the Marbled Baobab trees. His face was reptilian but had prominent features, similar to Calyx's white marbled eyes and his strong jawline. Malice was monstrous. He had four enormous muscular arms and tusks that protruded upward from his mouth. His breaths were strong, and his body positioned…focused. However, Adunai was not threatened, he enlarged in size to match Malice's stature. As Adunai enlarged his form he became mountainous. His fist quantified in size as they infused with granite, brass, and ivory directly from ElohI's grounds. Adunai stood as the first line of defense for the Elohii. Inaru stood next to Adunai. She absorbed light particles from the air which covered her entire form in a static shield. Her sight sharpened as did her fangs and talons as she stood second to Adunai. Malice smirked, then roared, "a challenge!"

As the Orishas and Elohii stood before the sanctuary, Okotadi and Atticus; part of the Destruction and Psyche's equal, entered invisibly and undetected behind the sanctuary. Okotadi knew the Elohii would assume a fair fight leaving him and Atticus a window to dispense unbalanced algorithms into the air. However, Hiyori was brilliant and knew to cover as much ground as possible. She placed a force field within the sanctuary as an additional layer of protection for the progeny. Okotadi filled the air with catalysts of depression, self-doubt, insanity, fear, and wrath. Inaru not underestimating Okotadi, knew he would release equations of iniquity. So, she placed countering methods and frequencies, to disrupt and cancel his equations. She used the Amore sent to cover the planet and the Elohii.

Although her defense helped the Orishas remain focused on the battle before them, a few more meteors were able to land and many Eliites rushed out, ready for battle. Okotadi glanced over at Inaru as he was reminded that she learned to perfect her potential from Anh Sang. Adunai aimed for Malice, as they ran towards one another, their bodies collided and the powerful impact from Adunai's mountainous form struck Malice out of ElohI and into her atmosphere where he pursued him and continued his fight. Psyche expelled poisonous vipers from her mouth as Mentira went for her sisters with razor daggered fingers. The Destruction had been unleashed upon ElohI. One of Okotadi's spores attempted to lure Alpha as she aimed to defend her sisters. Alpha found the deceptive thoughts to be overbearing as they whispered into her essence, "your parents left because they hated you...you are weak. Your sisters are going to die because of you..."as the sounds intensified in her mind, her sight began to blur.

Alpha: Shake it off, it's not real...it's not real. (heavily breathing)

She took several breaths then focused on the auras of her sisters. Being able to focus on their turquoise and rose quartz auras she was not only able to see them, but place shields around them. The shields were impenetrable, as its source was a gift from Pisim's light. Mentira, slashed her daggers wildly at the shield, but was unable to place her claws into the girls as hoped. Hiyori- Li, from her peripheral saw Mentira attacking the girls and upper palmed Mentira through the Knossos gardens to the east. One of Psyche's vipers slithered undetected, then surprisingly attacked Ogun...piercing its fangs into his legs. As the venom made its way up his leg, he fell over but managed to grab the reptile and tear its head from his body. After Hiyori-Li removed Mentira, she saw Ogun on the floor and black essence dripping from the bites. She then reached for her dagger and threw it over to Ogun. The gifts that Giza rained upon them were perfectly crafted for the encounter with the Destruction. Ogun melted the healing metal and inserted it through his wounds. The liquid metal made its way in and through Ogun fortifying his strength. Another viper made its way to him but was unable to pierce his form. The metal solidified, making him impenetrable. Vocal threw many jabs, upper cuts, and knock outs through as many Eliites that approached her. Ambrosia, lashed out her swords, splicing them into two, cutting down many Eliites as well. Okotadi not liking the odds of the battle began casting spells into the sanctuary attempting to break through the magnetic fields Hiyori placed as an additional layer of protection. After a few attempts, Okotadi and Atticus exerted spells upon the children that took immediate effect. Because of it, the Elohii, including the Orishas were weakened. They began to fall one by one, until Adunai, Inaru and Selu were the last standing. Malice had fallen back onto the lands along with Adunai and charged him with all of his might, but was unable to move Adunai with his fists, he was no match for the supreme lord's strength, especially when upon ElohI. Inaru was unable to cancel many of Okotadi and Atticus' algorithms, particularly with the weakened state of the Elohii and the progeny, so she attempted to plea with them...

Inaru: You need not do this

Atticus: Of course, we don't, but we will. My lord demands it

Okotadi: My quarrel is not with you my loves, but my brother. Once again, he has underestimated my intelligence. He will pay for his betrayal.

Adunai: Betrayal? You dare speak of it! You have damaged mother… murdered Anh Sang!!! (quivering) your very own equal! … simultaneously affecting Pisim! Affecting us All! You have taken our children Rhea and Calyx and turned them against us. You have taken a queen-mother and king-father away from their progeny!!! You are the essence of betrayal and corruption!

Okotadi: I loved Anh! but she meddled. And you have forgotten the image in which Rhea and Calyx were designed. They were made to execute My will! and shall follow the commandments that I have set before them. Never forget your place young god! You are in no position to question my methods!

Inaru: No place!? You are on our world! You have attacked OUR peace and OUR children! Where are they…Uncle? Where are Calyx and Rhea?! think of their children…

Mentira: He has, and we will do what mother and father expects us to, willingly!

Adunai: You will never win; my lord is greater than you

Okotadi: That he is…I cannot deny it, but he cannot endure the demise of his beloved children…can he now? I wish to remain balanced. To remain whole. And I have found a way that does not include Giza. I wish to revert the absence back to its original form. Now you both, will be the key to breaking Giza and maintaining the energy that sustains ME… check mate!

As Okotadi positioned himself to poison the auras of Inaru and Adunai as he had done to Calyx and Rhea, Giza inspired Selu, to act selflessly, "attack Okotadi and upon his destruction of your form, I will extract your essence to forge with Adunai and Inaru." Selu, looked over at her parents, "May you never rest and forever reign" then leaped over at Okotadi, hitting him twice in the face and pushing him backwards away from her lords. Adunai attempted to reach Selu, but Giza extracted him and Inaru placing them within his realm. Okotadi palmed Selu's crown, stopping her from advancing, then using his talons engraved a crater directly into Selu's head, removing her chakra. Okotadi then tossed Selu's lifeless form onto the ground.

Giza thought by allowing Adunai and Inaru to aid in the battle of the First, that the Elohii stood a chance, but he now saw that he had to allow enough time to pass before defeating Okotadi.

Okotadi yelled and sneered looking up to the sky. Disgust and saliva peered from his mouth…

Okotadi: Damn you brother!!! YOU HEAR THAT GIZA, GREAT MOVE BROTHER, HA! (laughing intensely). You removed them before I could… excellent move! It seems you have paid attention to all the times I wiped the grounds with you!!! It was excellent, I did not expect it. But I still have you by the All. I'll always be one step ahead. (He turns to the captured Elohii) Your Creators, your king even your queen have abandoned you. THEY have left you All to perish at my command. But, No! It's much to sinister. I will not be so cruel…You may continue to live as you have since the beginning of your existence. You will be drained and repurposed, yes. But it is I, that will command ElohI! She is mine to embrace, to indulge, to seduce, to control, to love, to possess. She will provide you with whatever you need. I'll see to it. Eliites, collect them. And place them into separate quadrants.

Oko, son of Ogun and Oya peered intensely ahead, speaking to the auras of his sisters and warrior Elohii…

Oko: I just want to smack him!

Quartz: Patience brother. It was right for Giza to remove our lords, had Okotadi destroyed them, he would most certainly have damaged Giza. Our Creator is wise, have faith.

Cocijo: Selu has been destroyed, my essence is saddened.

Quartz: Our sister is now with Giza. I know of it. Okotadi will pay for his treason.

Oko: We have to find a way to save the progeny, or they may decide to repurpose them first.

Ogun: Careful you wouldn't want someone to detect you communing with one another. Besides Okotadi will begin with us, to set an example for everyone else.

Psyche with her long serpent tongue detects the shift in Oko and Ogun's auras.

Psyche: My lord...

Okotadi: I… AM… SPEAKING!!! DO NOT…disrespect your lord.

Okotadi wondered what they would do if he repurposed chief Oko before them. The Elohii stood fast and focused with their energy towards Oko, as Okotadi lured his form forward. Okotadi, erected him for All to see. Then Okotadi's poisoned tongue, slipped into Oko's mouth and down to his heart where the viper struck repeatedly. Oko's essence leaked from his form. It poured from his eyes, nose, and fingertips. His body seized until it had been completely drained. The Elohii stood and watched, but to no avail there was not much they could do. Ogun stared at Okotadi with wrath and tears, but Okotadi did not pause until every ounce of essence was expelled, then tossed Oko's form before the feet of his father and the Elohii. Quartz and Ogun looked sharply into the eyes of Okotadi and demanded that he leave.

Quartz: You will not win! You are not worthy of being a Creator! You are lower than the redworms that dig beneath the mountains. My gods are mighty... I will avenge my brother! I will rip your tongue from your form and watch happily... as it turns on you!

Okotadi sneered at Quartz's words, thinking the emptying of Oko would've saddened them, but instead they All focused the potential they had left and peered at Okotadi with contempt.

I found myself tossing and turning, trying to wake my body up. I sat up quickly, sweat dripping from my face and down my chin. My shirt was soaking wet. I got up, went to take a shower, then sat on the edge of the bed reflecting on my dream. I sat there for about 10 minutes or so, then Elegua greeted me, "Leslie". I turned around and saw him standing in my room. I stood up instantly while staring at him as my hand slid slowly over to my forearm and I pinched it, "I can't feel that... yes"!

Leslie: Where have you been? I've been thinking that I'm crazy.

Elegua: There is such a thing as time passed and time yet to come. I exist in a place where they coincide. Sometimes we must return to the past to have an effect on the moving present.

Leslie: The moving present?

Elegua: The future... Your final dream. What was it about?

Leslie: The taking of the Elohii and the removal of Adunai and Inaru. It looked like he was gonna repurpose the captured Elohii.

Elegua: It is time. I need you to be very still

Elegua stepped very close to me, informing me to be still, but as he stepped closer, I backed up. I wasn't sure what to do. I backed up but ran out of space to continue backing up. I stood there and he said, "breathe". I wasn't convinced and could not calm down fast enough that Elegua, placed his palm on my head.

As his hand touched my head there was this violet color light between us. Then he showed me what he had in his hand, and it was a small purple crystal.

Leslie: Uh…did that just come out of my head?

He took the gem and placed it inside of small suede looking bag with drawstrings.

Elegua: The Destruction have figured out Giza's next move. They will begin searching for you. Every few decades, they search for the line of prophets, descendants of the Elohii, of the first children, the Orishas. You are a descendant from Ogun and Oya's, but also share existence with the will of Inaru. I have removed the essence from your crown. This will make it hard for them to see you when they arrive in this lifetime. Under no circumstance must you remove the amethyst quartz from the bag… only if instructed by me or someone of higher rank.

Leslie: Higher rank? wait… the Destruction is after me? What the fuck did I do?... when do you think they'll make a visit? Do you have a date? Time?

Elegua: I do not, but we are upon final days. You must unleash the Awakening.

Elegua grabbed my arm, turned my right palm over, placed my palm to his mouth and started speaking in a foreign language. As the words left his mouth, they began to engrave themselves onto my body. I could not decipher the lettering nor the words, but the foreign language he spoke saturated my body.

Elegua: The decree has been delivered. You cannot run from this Leslie. It is your job to bring forth the end. This is the lifetime where we bring about the beginning.

I jumped up out of my sleep, with my heart pounding. I stood there for a few minutes, contemplating once again another dream. I couldn't believe the dreams that I kept having. As I went over to the mirror to engage with myself and convince myself that "I am not losing my mind", I noticed the small bag sitting on my drawer and tats all over my arms and neck. I slid my right hand over to my left forearm and pinched myself... looked into the mirror and square in the eyes, "oh shit, I can feel that".

13. Encounter

Anchorwoman Henry: "It's been several months since the Martial Reform under the COVID-19 pandemic crisis. President Donaldson assured the nation on March 4, 2020, that enacting the reform was for the safety of its citizens. As a measure the National Guard has been mobilized to keep citizens off the streets and out of harm's way until Congress along with the CDC has implemented methods on controlling the spread of the virus. However, the presence of the National Guard has stirred episodic riots particularly during the protests in Miami, FL regarding the execution of Antwan Pearson on May 16, 2020. Pearson, 18 years old at the time of death, was yet another case of mistaken identity in the past year, when local law enforcement brutally took down the victim in daylight. Pearson was said to have been connected in a series of armed robberies and home invasions. As it turns out the victim neither fit the descriptions that have come to light recently nor has Pearson been placed at any of the crime scenes. The victim's family, friends, and community have rallied to mourn and protest the young man's death. But the presence of the National Guard, enforced with upholding the Martial Reform and its curfews, has caused tension among the protesters. Local officials, community members, family and even a few celebrities are refusing to uphold the reform until justice on behalf of Pearson along with so many others have been handled. Earlier this week, Pearson's mother Michelle, provided the following statement, "This is unacceptable! I am beyond words, beyond pain! They had no right, no right whatsoever to remove my son from this Earth! To remove him from me! I didn't even get the chance to watch him grow, get married and make a long life for himself. These fucking coward ass officers, demons with badges!... had no motherfucking right! I am beyond furious! I am beyond tears! I feel like someone put their hands through my chest and ripped... my heart... out! MY SON was not yours for the taking! He was not yours to do as you please with! He was MINE... to love and take care of... my beautiful Antwan, was profiled, followed, and murdered by the same officers that swore oaths to protect and serve our community, not rob us of our children. So, I swear an oath also, to not move from these streets (crowd amped up in background) until justice has been delivered! I pray that God rains down a punishment on every last one of you cold blooded sorry motherfuckers! ... with something fierce!" Anchorwoman Henry continues, "Pearson's death sparked a series of marches that have heightened over the past six months, across various states where others executed under mistaken identity have taken place as well. It's no secret that the social injustices for Black and Latino communities have worsened, particularly under the COVID-19 restriction and Martial Reform. President Donaldson has not issued a statement

133

regarding the outcry of the nation. Leniency from chief of police Ruiz on police accountability has also been an enabling factor, as a significant increase of racialized hate groups along with liberal militia, upholding their own versions of the Martial Reform also heightened. Many have taken matters into their own hands and the results have been fatal. In the last six months alone South Florida, Chicago, parts of Alabama, Washington D.C., California, Georgia, New York, New Jersey, Louisiana, and the Carolinas have a combined death toll in the hundreds and rising. My heart shatters as I report that amongst the hundreds dead, 35%... 35% are under the age of eighteen" ...

I didn't mean to watch the news, but I hit the remote by mistake when I sat on the bed. My body ran cold with the news. I could not help but fall to my knees and pray. Tears poured down my face, for the young man robbed of his future and to all the parents that will never hold their children again. My stomach knotted up; I could not help but become enraged. "Elegua!!! Where are you?!!!" I haven't heard from Elegua in over two years. I'm starting to think that maybe I hallucinated him all along, but the foreign language tatted on my body that glowed from time to time was proof that I hadn't. All I know is that I needed more protection in case the gods forgot about me.

I made it over to Kevin's Guns and Such, I glanced through the various selections of protection. Until now I'd been afraid to acquire a pistol because I truly don't ever want to be put into a situation where I'd have to shoot, or worst kill someone. As the sales lady walked over, I spotted the gun I could see myself pulling the trigger to.

Roulette: I see you glaring at that heater

Leslie: Yea. I'm not really educated on guns, but I want something intimidating, but not too show offy.

Roulette: Well for starters you're looking at the Magnum .44 Desert Eagle. It's a revolver and an excellent weapon to put a hole through someone. So, who you looking to kill?

Leslie: Uuummm, no one in particular, but with reality being what it is, I gotta protect me and mine.

Roulette: I hear that. Well, you have excellent taste. But let's start you off with something that won't fracture your wrist. I always say your first instinct is normally the right choice. Except for with men. The third decision is normally right, at least that's been my experience. So, let's try my first instinct for you. This here is a Ruger, its compact, lightweight, and powerful. Plus, there's a sale happening. Buy a .380 and get the shells 50% off.

Leslie: Can I hold it, or do you need my ID first?

Without hesitation or checking my identification, this really nice lady took the gun out and placed it on the display case before me…

Roulette: Here you are. Now when you pick it up you wanna be confident in your grip. You ever held a gun before?

Leslie: Do guns at the arcade count? I'm really good at killing zombies

Roulette: Yea, that does count, but let me show you…

As she picked up the gun, she showed me the correct way to do so. Then handed it over to me. As she told me the specs about the gun, I noticed the joy on her face…she seemed to enjoy her job, really liked guns or both.

Leslie: You really know a lot about guns.

Roulette: Yea, my ancestry is rooted in this land and warfare. My great great grandfather is Lakota Sioux as is my great great grandmother. By the time you get to my grandparents they were defenders of our tradition and killers of anything White (chuckled). My parents, brothers and cousins were all part of a militia-based team, well actually they still are. However, they became a little too preoccupied with protecting us that over time they became a little prejudice and extremely overprotective. Not me though, I left, traveled, went to community college, and have friends of every race. Shit, my kid's dad is blackish. When I came home, they wanted me to denounce everyone I met, or I had the option to outcast myself. So, I live here and sell guns to people.

As the conversation deepened, there was a tattoo on the sales lady's neck that resembled one on my shoulder. I didn't mention anything because I don't know who to trust, plus who would believe my experiences of late. I've been trying to convince myself that it happened from time to time. As she told me her life story, I felt as if she needed friends...

Leslie: I'm Leslie by the way.

Roulette: Roulette. I know, the odds that I'd love guns and sell them. My parents sent me on the right path when naming me. Wanna know something funny? I named my daughter Wesson and my puppy Gage.

As we both laughed, I made the anti-antisocial decision to give her my number. She seems like someone I'd hangout with and she has military experience which is a plus.

As I left the store, feeling empowered because I was now the owner over a Ruger LCP .380, that I named Makaveli for obvious reasons, I noticed big oddly stripes of clouds in the sky and an instant change in the weather. The wind picked up severely and the sky turned into a hot pink-orange color. As I drove off and made a right onto Capital Circle N.E. I had to come to a sudden stop. There were people exiting their vehicles and running in a panic. I stopped, got out of my car to see what was happening. My gaze went straight to the cloud that looked like a fist with the index finger pointed straight up. It was so lifelike. I could see the wrinkles in the skin and the fibers within the nail. The longer I stared the more naturally detailed the cloud became. As I broke my glance, I looked at the cloud next to it... it was the palm of a hand, extremely detailed as well. "What the fuck?" As I did an extremely obvious 360, there were clouds in every direction with various hand symbols, like if the sky was throwing up gang signs, shit there was even one with a middle finger! The longer I looked my head started spinning, not like the exorcist, but like the room was spinning. The tattoos on my left arm began to glow, the wind and cloud images began to merge together. I had that stuck feeling all over again, like my birthday night two and a half years ago. Thunder rang loudly that it set car alarms off. The sky banged and pounded rhythmically. My head continued to spin; my eyes could no longer focus. The wind picked up even more, so I did the only rational thing, I got back in my car... at least that's what I assumed I did. Yep, you guessed it... I was back in that damn cave. Except, this time it looked different.

Elegua stood there but didn't even give me a second to come to. He didn't even greet me, and his permanent friendly smile was not on his face. He immediately placed his fist upon his forehead and his other hand over my heart. I could feel a surge of energy between us.

However, this energy seemed livelier. As I allowed my consciousness to connect to the Amore, I remember feeling completely unattached from my body, for this is the deepest I have ever been within myself. Once the floating sensation ended, I could see various spots of light, almost like colorful balls of lightning evenly spaced down an extremely long corridor. Each spot of light had a person standing before it ever so intently…watching these electric spheres as if something was supposed to occur. As Elegua guided me down the hallway, he said nothing. But I had a million questions, like one… where is my body? Because I was actually driving down the street… well technically I was parked, but in the street, nonetheless. But since he didn't say anything and seemed to be serious, I kept it to myself. Although I'm pretty sure he could read my thoughts. As we walked on, the people standing guard in front of the colorful balls seemed familiar. I felt like I was literally walking down a history lesson. The last person to my left I would know anywhere and I kinda wanted to stop, hug him, and ask him for his autograph, but Elegua signaled with his hand to keep up, then finally, we stopped. We reached an eye. This eye wasn't like an eyeball, but a floating shimmering, see through symbolic eye. It looked like it was made from fairy dust, but of course that would be retarded because fairies don't exist. Elegua looked at me, "Really, Fairy dust"? I was immediately embarrassed, I knew he was listening, but didn't think I'd get called out for it.

However, I did notice this was the only floating glowing thing that didn't have someone stalking it. "Your time has come", Elegua telepathically stated and gestured that I enter the eye...

You've heard the phrase, "I've died and gone to heaven", well minus the dead part (fingers crossed), I just might be in heaven. As I stepped into the light, no pun intended, I appeared upon a road. I started on this path, every step I took, people started to appear on opposite sides. They all kneeled as I passed as if I was royalty or something. After maybe forty steps I came upon a small village. I continued on the path and came across faces I knew, faces I loved. Faces I never thought that I would look upon again! The first face made joy sweep through me and tears stream down my cheeks. As I approached, I embraced my abuela so tightly. I never thought that I would see her again, let alone hold her. Although deep within my conscience, I felt every emotion and memory attached to her. This moment was everything and for a few seconds I could care less about some mission. I could've remained in her arms for the rest of my life and been totally fine with not ever moving. As I released her, she didn't say a word, but somehow, what was not said was completely understood. Everything I needed to know came with that smile and hug. I stepped back on the road, blew her a kiss and she kneeled before me. With the next step another familiar face. My grandma Yoya stood there ever so proudly. Her posture was fierce! I approached and kneeled before her. Her hand caressed my face and motioned me to rise…

Grandma: A queen only kneels before god

Leslie: Grandma you look good…

Grandma: and you look ready darling. Goh'on…

I stepped back and she kneeled so proudly before me. This village of women is my ancestry! I embrace both my cousin Coko and my aunt Rosie even my mamacita was there! Continuing on the path I stood before the person I've wanted to see the most. My mom, standing there with the biggest brightest smile on her face, "mija" she held her arms out and I dove right into them. I squeezed her like my life depended on it. I was in pure shock! I was in joy! So much so that I wanted to tell her everything and yet nothing came out. Only tears and the pounding of my heart was all that I could communicate. She wiped my face, "I am so proud of you… mira lo Annunaki. Te dije que they were real", we both bust out laughing so hard. I could've stayed there listening to her laugh, but she led me before these very large and gorgeous beings. As I watched her walk off, she too kneeled. These Annunaki, as my mom called them shun brightly. I did not expect to be here before them. I was in such awe. I can't really explain it, but these gods and goddesses before me seemed to be made from whatever the universe is made out of. They had suns, moons, stars and water for eyes and skin. Their attire was fire, earthen, sky type clothing. They were decked out in all sorts of jewels, feathers, and elements. I just stared at them, but one thing I noticed… I wasn't scared. As they all sat before me upon their thrones, looking directly at me, in unison they greeted me...

The Orishas: Order and Love, my Queen

Leslie: Hey!

Ogun: Allow me. I am Ogun and this is my equal Oya, we are images of Giza. This is Kuei-Shen and Hiyori-Li images of Anh Sang. Cocijo and Selu images of Pisim. We are the very first Elohii, children of the planet Elohī and heirs to the First children of Origen King god Adunai and Queen god Inaru. We are known as the Orisha.

Leslie: I remember seeing some of your life during the beginning. What about the images of Okotadi?

Kuei-Shen: Our brother Calyx and sweet sister Rhea were stolen and tricked by him. Then repurposed into Titans upon the aftermath that became Origen. He renamed them Adam and Eve. They then bore cainabels (Destruction); devours and destroyers of their own kind. They are responsible for breeding the Eliites. The Eliite army was also comprised of repurposed Elohii. Their lineage is responsible for the iniquities which affects humanity. Menitra and Malice together are responsible for slavery, brutality, and punishment of all types while

142

Psyche and Atticus are responsible for the seven plagues: hate, greed, lust, wrath, filth, untruths and pain.

Leslie: Elegua took a jewel out of my head and said that I may be in some trouble

Oya: Yes. The Eliites execute leaders, prophets, and messengers, but more importantly Elohii. Their job is to maintain the death of humanity which in return fuels Okotadi, he aims to become the final Creator source.

Leslie: So, you are telling me that I am going to die?!

Selu: Throughout time Okotadi has figured out our approach to bringing him down and so, he has sent the Titans and their Eliites to destroy the descendants of Giza and to ensure his reign.

Leslie: On the way in, I saw people from my history. I even saw the dog himself, DMX… is this heaven?

Oya: They are timekeepers. Prophets and messengers. Even in death they still remain as watchers. Since Inaru and Adunai were assigned with weakening Okotadi through time, this he has figured out, therefore we have watchers to help regulate the portals. Also, no this is not heaven. We are within the deepest level of your conscience. This place is built from your ancestral connection, memories, and past and future self.

Hiyori- Li: Messengers, prophets, and leaders alike... many of them died at the hands of Eliites, before being able to deliver their decree. Some were murdered, others fell weak to the sins of humanity and became distracted in their task. The Destruction have invented and implemented various techniques to keep the strong down and unaware of their essence. Okotadi has even enslaved our home planet. ElohI was repurposed, Earth's new function keeps the essence of our descendants bound by the algorithms and equations casted by Okotadi. We have had to wait a very long time to assign the Awakening. If delivered while the Destruction are awaiting it, then they'd know how to counter it and we would not be able to regenerate our supreme Creator Giza.

Leslie: So, I have to deliver the Awakening? By myself?... What should I do and how do I do it, cause I don't want to die! At least not before being 99 years old.

Cocijo: Your reality is not what you think. We are all but energy and matter. Yes, we are connected to people, places, and things, but the battle for the survival of the essence of life itself must be preserved. If Okotadi succeeds, then the possibility for the presence of light and the presence of sound will cease to exist permanently!

Leslie: The Am?

Cocijo: Precisely. Okotadi does not understand that he is being driven by the absence, Infinitus. His eternal function is to be without.

Kuei-Shen: Careful in how you speak Cocijo, she is mortal. Leslie, you will not die; we will ensure it. But your time for sacrifice will come. Your essence is different from other messengers and leaders. You are a prophet because your lineage returns back to us. You descend from Ogun and Oya's line. But Inaru and Adunai's essence was distributed across lifetimes. You have inherited Inaru's essence for your time. You are ordained through cosmic energy for this mission. Turn around... The people before you are all parts of your ancestry, as are we. They have been waiting for your lifetime to reunite. They will provide you with their strength and love.

Leslie: Wait... so am I gonna have superpowers?!

Ogun: In a manner of speaking. Those who no longer live in your world, but live eternally, will channel their essence through you. You will need to be strong, for the power you will receive can overwhelm and even distract you from your course. To ensure success, you will need to become balanced.

Leslie: Ok. So, what do I need to do? Clearly, I meditate, I also do yoga. I still eat meat tho, should... I like... become vegan?

The Orishas looked amongst themselves in laughter, for Leslie's naiveté they found amusing.

Cocijo: You will meet your equal and share your energy with him. Once this happens it will awaken him and together you will both be strong enough to balance the hate you will encounter.

Ogun: You saw the beginning. Everything is paired with feminine and masculine energy. Even the initial absence and presence of existences. Okotadi is completely off balance because he murdered Anh. His logic is blinded, and he is unable to function in the way he should, this is why he can't spread the imbalance himself. He needs the paired Destruction. Leslie, trust in what lives within you, it is forever pure, forever loving, forever peaceful.

I smiled and bowed before the Orishas and walked back towards the eye. As my ancestry appeared upon entrance they faded upon exit. As I reached the end of the eye portal, turned around and the Orishas blew their happiness at me as I exited.

Elegua: Haha! I can feel your power! Look at you, you've been marked with allegiance. How was it? I want to know everything...

Leslie: Well, I saw my mom and grandmothers... The Orishas were pretty cool. This was, by far, the coolest thing ever! I have to deliver the Awakening...

Elegua: The Awakening! Then it truly has begun.

Leslie: O, by the way, do you happen to know who my equal is?

Elegua: Trust in what lives within you

Leslie: That's the same thing Orisha Ogun said. I guess I'll just have to ask Drake to marry me then...

Elegua: Who is Drake?

I looked over at Elegua with both a look of disgust and bewilderment. And as I was about to answer, horns were blowing for me to move my car. I stepped out and onto the street, but the sky was a normal blue. There was nothing mysterious or apocalyptic as I remembered. "Get your fat ass out the road!" I stuck my middle finger to the bald dude in the pickup truck behind me, "go around stupid", I got back in my car and headed home.

14. Revive

Okotadi paced and paced and paced as he murmured to himself… "I can't believe those Elohii. I gave them a choice to follow me! A true god… (sucks his teeth) I am no Creator? What do they know?... I should repurpose the function of all Elohii warriors, those female types think their powerful because Oya is their matriarch. I should've emptied her first! (Exhales) What is Giza up to? He surprised me by removing Adunai and Inaru. He even sacrificed one of their kin, to save his precious heirs… and the Elohii love him and think that HE… is worthy! He is a fool…although he has deceived me. So, what is Giza up to? Where did he hide them?... More than likely on his "pure realm" (mockingly), he knows that I can no longer enter… nor do I want to, if the opportunity presents itself! It is there that I must send the Destruction… but they may not be permitted to enter either. Hmmm… what are you up to brother?" The more Okotadi paced and thought out loud, the deeper the grooves upon the ground became. He walked about for months contemplating his maneuvers, until he finally answered his own question… "I know! He won't try to stop me head on, that coward wouldn't dare look me in the eyes! He will deceive me once again. He won't return back to ElohI, but later when he feels that I would've forgotten. It is rather brilliant, but he will never be ahead of me. I must act". Once Okotadi solved his inquiry, he hadn't been aware that he'd walked so deeply into the undergrounds of Origen. "Where, exactly… have I…?" As Okotadi glanced around at the various layers and sediment of the planetess, he was enlightened. "Ha! It's too brilliant. Brother could never outthink me! He thinks that he is going to just wait it out, the stupidity! I will repurpose all of ElohI, then those born unto her at any moment in time, will forget their true nature. I will pace caverns into her layers, I will spread venom into her streams… into her essence. She will bend to my will. She will be ElohI no more, but the earth upon which my greatness will be realized! Brother will never suspect it. Giza's too noble to think at such depths". Okotadi immediately called out to Calyx and Rhea. He wanted to let them know of his amazing new idea.

Calyx: My Lord

Rhea: Have you reached a resolution?

Okotadi: I have. No need to continue repurposing the Elohii. I am now aware that it is an ineffective use of potential. As a matter of fact, there is no longer the need. We will repurpose ElohI. She will do in time what we need. Our potential is better spent casting equations to predict Giza's movements.

Calyx: Masterful. Then the Elohii and Giza can pay for their betrayal…indefinitely.

Rhea: What are our orders?

Okotadi: The repurposing of the planet will take the Elohii of Giza. Without Adunai's whereabouts, they will need to do the initial work. Separate them, then bind them. Place the male type in the caves and caverns... they will dig unto they reach ElohI's core. The female types will remove and gather the debris and the Elohii of Giza will use the removed material to build totems and monuments. These relics must be made specifically of ivory, gold, marble, and jade. The lavender quartz if you find any, give them to me, along with all topaz gems. These relics will serve as points of focus where we can channel our potential.

Rhea: What of the Destruction?

Calyx: Atticus and Psyche can serve you best my Lord. Malice and Mentira can maintain the order of the Elohii. We can divide the Eliites, they can assist as well.

Okotadi: I couldn't have said it better. We know what to do. Let us move, as this will take time. But first, your potential must mimic that of what I must do.

Rhea and Calyx: Honor and order, my Lord!

Okotadi recalled the moment from both Calyx and Rhea of their initial encounter. As he watched himself empty and repurpose Rhea's potential first, he granted her the function to breed cainabels, devours and destroyers of the Elohii kind. He ordained that their progeny would produce Eliites, anti Elohii. After Rhea, shared her potential with Calyx and they both reawakened to their new function, he renamed them. Calyx was now Adam, first father of Earth. Rhea was now Eve, first mother of Earth. As Okotadi replaced their memory impacting the moving present, the function of the Destruction itself fell in line with his new strategy.

Giza felt the shift. He knew that Okotadi could not refrain from ensuring his success and this was the exact moment that Giza waited for. After removing both Adunai and Inaru he placed them in the stillness of his eternal realm, within the Amore. Selu's sacrifice granted him the opportunity to do so, but also used Selu's compassion, love, and glory to grant Selu chief goddess of resurrections, which would prove effective in the next phase of his plan. Giza remembered the Am's caution and instruction to carry out the mission through lifetimes. If he is to win against Okotadi, then he must be able to revive Adunai and Inaru upon every sacrifice, then they can be reborn again until Okotadi is vulnerable enough to rebalance.

Giza: Awaken, my loves

Adunai: Selu! Where is Selu?

Selu: I live father

Adunai and Inaru both embraced Selu and planted kisses and affection upon her.

Inaru: How has this happened?

Giza: I prepared Selu to do what was honorable. She sacrificed her essence for your survival. I knew Okotadi would view it as a scheme, but unyielding sacrifice and love, creates opportunities that my dear brother cannot account for. His logic and madness cannot fathom reason.

Selu: Without hesitation (places both hands upon her crown)

Giza: I knew Okotadi could not resist in changing time. Therefore, I have been waiting in silence for him to make his move. And now that he has, Selu is now goddess of revival. A reaction to his repurposing of Rhea as first mother, but initially mother of death. Selu's potential will cover your successions across lifetimes.

Inaru: Rhea's the mother of death? My beautiful girl...

Giza: Calyx and Rhea are now Adam and Eve, it is through them that iniquity and chaos are able to exist. We will provide a moment of silence to honor who they were, but we will not hesitate in preparing for who they are.

Selu, Adunai and Inaru in unison: Honor and order!

Inaru: What do you require of us?

Giza: I will extract your essence. Selu will remain here with me. I along with the Amore will spread your potential across the moments where I am at my weakest. It is here where you must find one another, adhere to the decree needed within that lifetime and act. The weaker I become, the harder it will be for you both across time, to remember your potential and task. This is why Selu will remain here, keeping an eye on you, always.

Adunai: Why will you be weak father? You seem to be strong now, why don't we act now!

Giza: It is now that we will act. As I spread part of my potential to be with you, I am not sure of the attempts you will need to fully weaken Okotadi. I was instructed by the Am, that it had to be through lifetimes, and I must obey. After I cast you both, I must remove my crown to make future Elohii aware of your transitions. I will use as much potential necessary to ensure your connection, but I must remain here in silence and complete focus as this act will strain much of my essence.

Adunai: Masterful... Then the Eliites and Okotadi can pay for their betrayal...indefinitely.

Selu: With my newfound essence, I can watch over the ancestry. This way upon their sacrifice, win or lose, they can keep watch along with me. Okotadi will sooner or later comprehend what we have done.

Inaru: Brilliant. So, it is up to us Adunai, to ensure we connect. I say send us to when you are at your weakest upon ElohI. Selu, give us all that you can.

Giza: I will be close to extinction, during your final lifetime. This will be an extremely hard task for you. It is here where too much time would've passed, and life will be saturated in the destructive order of Okotadi and his Titans. Please understand that Okotadi, would've repurposed ElohI…she is now Earth and bends to the essence of the Destruction. Adunai's connection to her will be repelled.

Adunai: How could such madness exist! I am exhausted of uncle… I am exhausted of Okotadi! ElohI…repurposed… how is that even possible? Wouldn't he need my help?

Giza: He has all of our Elohii now and forever. Your connection will be distorted more than Inaru's because of it. You must try with all your essence to remember. Things will change drastically once I enact it all.

Selu: I've got you father, no matter how many revivals it takes. I got you!

Giza: Remove all doubt, have faith…

Adunai turns to Inaru… "I don't believe… I refuse to believe that I could ever forget you".

Inaru: We do not know what we are up against. We've lost mother and Anh. We've lost our planet, our children, their progeny. All that father speaks is real. But I know indefinitely… that I could never forget you! Even if I have to fight you to remember me or love me, it is what I will do! Even if it takes forever…

As they all came into an agreeance with the plan of action, they gathered together and offered moments of silence for what was lost. After sighs, tears and heartfelt expressions were shared, Adunai extended Inaru's palm towards his lips and placed words of remembrance into her hand. His words then carved themselves upon her form. "Forget me not" as he kissed her lovingly, then placed her hand upon his heart. "Go on, take it", Adunai encouraged Inaru to remove his heart chakra. Inaru with slight hesitation, "isn't it better if you keep it"?

Adunai: It seems that you would have better use for it. You must find me, I'm hoping this way, your pull to me, regardless of the lifetime, will be even stronger, whether you initially remember me or not. You can give it back to me, later.

Inaru: I could never forget you

Adunai: This will guarantee that you never will

Inaru, with her hand over Adunai's heart, extracted his love for her and merged it with hers. They then embraced for a final time. Giza then extracted Adunai and Inaru completely into the Amore portal and spoke the words… "May the energy that sustains you, never rest and forever reign". The decree manifested and shelled the heirs. Waiting for the moment when their essence would be needed. Giza removed his eye, placing it into Selu's palm then he planted and rooted himself still focusing the remainder of the All's potential across time.

15. Remember

It was Monday August 23, 1999, and I did not want to go to school. Typically, on tv shows senior year is supposed to be the most amazing time in anyone's life but I particularly did not like school. I wanted my parents to send me to American High school, but of course they never listen, so I've been at Carol City and have just about hated every moment of it, except for tenth grade, that year was actually pretty cool. As I sat in the living room trying to watch as much X-Men as possible while wolfing down a bowl of Froot Loops, my sister J of course was taking her precious time in the bathroom fixing her hair. Part of me was complaining deep inside because I hated being late to anything, but the outside part of me who loved the Sinister Island episodes and cereal had no complaint except that I wouldn't be able to finish the episode because we had to leave in ten minutes. As my mom headed towards the door, "vamonos", I turned the t.v. off, grabbed my backpack and got in the car. This would be the first time that me and both my sisters would be at the high school at the same time since Vee was now in the 9th grade. As my mom dropped us off, I took a look at my schedule and headed for the worst subject known to man, English. The closer I got to the room, the slower I walked. I got to the door, but before entering, I placed my schedule back into my folder and then my folder back into my backpack… I took a deep breath walked in, and then it happened. I saw the boy that could make all my hopes and dreams come true. I never even made it fully to the teacher's desk but lingered in the doorway a little longer as I stared at this extremely gorgeous dude. I shook it off, walked over to the teacher. As she spoke, "take a look at the seating chart and pick a seat… this is where you'll sit for the entire school year". I couldn't believe my ears… today was the best day at school! I finally understood why senior year is the best time of anyone's life. I looked at the chart and saw the name above all other names, Bellamy Kalloway. I looked at the name, then looked at him, double checked that I was correct and then chose the desk across from him. The teacher wrote down my name and then I headed over to my seat. As I sat down, he looked at me, "what's up" … I said, "hello", but my heart was pounding like the well-dressed wolf in heat from Looney Tunes. On the outside I was as quiet as a church mouse. Oh, but in my heart fireworks and wedding bells burst and rang ever so loudly! This was too much excitement for an introvert such as myself to handle… if I had eaten two bowls of Froot Loops this morning, I'd clearly be having a stroke right now! As the morning bell rang more students poured in and other students eventually filled the extra desks in our group, but for the rest of that class period and to my knowledge we were the only two people in the room.

As the day ended, I got home, I changed my clothes and went straight for the t.v. to enjoy the afternoon cartoon line up. I fried two bolognas, toasted some bread, made me two sandwiches, gathered two bananas and a cup full of juice and camped out on the couch until 5 pm. Afterwards, I barricaded myself in my room with DMX lyrically exhibiting my teenage rage. I could not help but think about Bellamy Kalloway as I prepped my clothes for the following days. He was beautiful, tall, well dressed. I should've sat next to him, so I could've inhaled him all class period. After organizing my clothes, I sat down to attempt the first day assignments, but it became a little hard to focus on homework, so I stood up, turned my radio up as loud as possible and rapped along, "…If you love the money then prepare to die for it, niggas done started something…don't come at me with no bullshit use caution, cause when I wet shit, I dead shit, like abortions for bigger portions, of extortions and racketeering, got niggas fearing, fuck what you heard, it's what you hearing"… my mother knocked on my door loudly and opened it up "mirame, baja! esa basura"… and just as quickly as she had opened the door she closed it back shut. Now how was I supposed to get this dude off my mind and focus on my homework if I couldn't get this song off my chest!

As my senior year slowly passed by, all I could do is stare at this guy every Monday, Wednesday, and Friday during first period. It was the only part of the school day I looked forward to… actually that's a lie, and fifth period, I loved math and my teacher Mr. Torres taught it really well. Then the day came where all my staring at Bellamy paid off and he asked me for my number. Granted he did so in front of all the other boys that sat in our group, but I did not care and wrote it down in his notebook as requested. We eventually hung out and made out a few times, but he never made it to the end of senior year. Two months before graduation he stopped coming to school. I tried calling Bellamy to find out what happened, but he never gave me an answer.

An entire year and a half had passed. Me and Bellamy had lost touch. It wasn't until one day I found myself bored so I decided to clean my room, when I stumbled across my old address book. I opened it up, looking at all the different telephone numbers I had and by the time I got to the Ks, there it was, Bellamy Kalloway's cell phone and conveniently his house number. I called the house number and he answered. We spoke briefly, then he asked, "can I come by and see you?" Trying not to sound too excited, "umm, yea… you can." He came over later that night about 7pm and we stood outside my dad's house just talking about everything that had happened since he left school. "Yea my pops grounded me for getting into some shit, with these niggas, plus my grades were no good. I had to do summer school to graduate, so that's why I left." I could watch this man all day. After he shared with me, what had taken place in his life I guess it was my turn… "I have a baby. I had a little boy a few months ago. You wanna see him?" He looked at me shockingly, replied, "who's the father? And yea, of course". We walked into my room as I showed him my little light skinned baby that was knocked out in his crib with his mouth wide opened. As we walked back outside, I answered him, "remember I was in karate, right? So, that dude who I said would not leave me alone. It's his baby, but he ain't around anymore and I don't want to talk about it." He shook his head, "that's messed up, how he just gonna leave you and his jit?" Without hesitation, "I honestly don't care because he was getting on my nerves anyways, plus I get to have my son all to myself, so it kinda works out." After I got that off my chest, our conversation that night turned into us vibing for the next three years.

One night he picked me up and we headed to our main hangout, lifeguard tower #9 over at Hallandale Beach. We sat up there so many nights just kicking the shits, but this night was different. As our chit chat came to a pause, we both sat in enjoyable silence watching the waves breathe onto the shore. The moon sat in the night sky so full, so bright. And for the first time in my young life, I felt complete. Although Bell was not my son's father or technically "my man", he was at this moment my world, my equal.

Leslie: What do you see?

Bellamy: I see the ocean, waves hitting the sand, the moon... and the fact that you need a pedicure.

Leslie: Whatever!

Bellamy: What do you see?

Leslie: Possibility. I see us, sitting on our thrones. Look around, there's no one in sight, except for us. The view before us is endless and totally ours. We aren't bound by any limitations.

Bellamy: I love your mind. You always get deep with it.

Leslie: Even the moon tonight, she's so full, lighting the ocean and perhaps our way to something more.

As these words left my lips, it was almost as if the moon heard me. Because a few minutes later the clouds that shrouded her moved and we were in her spotlight.

Bellamy: I think she's encouraging us...

Leslie: Encouraging, what?

Just then, Bell looked at me as if he was seeing me for the first time. I simply couldn't believe that my love at first sight was actually here with me in this beautiful and almost perfect scene. "Croney, I gotta tell you something", he signaled with his finger that I move a little closer. Bell placed his hand on my cheek, ever so softly then kissed me. Although we've made out plenty of times, there was something really different about tonight, I just didn't know what it was. I looked at him, "that's so interesting, keep talking", he grabbed me, placing me right over his lap. He embraced and slowly caressed my back and lower back. He kissed my lips, cheeks, nose, and forehead, then made his way back to my lips and neck. A few moments later we were on lifeguard tower #9 making love under moonlight. It was unlike anything I had experienced. He whispered, "can I keep you?" I didn't reply with words but pulled him closer to me with my right leg across the back of his waist. We were so engaged with one another, that it truly seemed that we were the only two people on the planet, our planet, making love on our throne. We laid there for while looking upon one another in enjoyable silence. We then dressed and sat there a while longer. "Are you ready?", he said, but the glow on the ocean caught my attention. "Look", the moonlight seemed to almost create a partition on the ocean. Bellamy stood up quickly, "Oh shit." I then stood up after him…

Leslie: What do you think that is?

Bellamy: I'm not sure

Leslie: Should we take a closer look or haul ass?

Bellamy: Nah, let's go see

Leslie: If we die, I'm gonna kill you!

As we exited the safety of the lifeguard tower we walked closer to the water. I held onto Bell's arm, and we inched forward, but our inching forward along with the immense glow made it hard to see how far out we'd actually walked. Bellamy seemed to be completely enchanted by the moon's light, but my anxiety and slight paranoia was more skeptical. We walked on until I noticed the lifeguard tower was quite a way behind us.

Leslie: B, how are we this far out in the ocean and not wet?

Bellamy: I don't know, but don't jinx us.

The glowing partition stopped. A doorway opened before us. Bellamy looked at me as I looked at him. He placed his hand in mine, "we ride together, we die together", I instantly responded, "boy shut your ass up", we both laughed, took deep breaths, and walked through the door.

I sat up from this dream feeling weird. After I moved to Tallahassee back in 2004, Bellamy and I communicated briefly, but then fell off completely. When I moved, I told myself that I would go to school, graduate, move back to the crib, land a great job making bank and that Bell would marry me, and we'd live happily ever after. But as reality would have it, I fucked school up, was too immature and undisciplined with both jobs and men and that the following ten years

164

would actually be a struggle because I didn't know how to be an adult.

A few days after that dream, I could not stop thinking about it and Bell. I sat there aimlessly starring out the window at the rain folding laundry, going over every inch of that dream. But the weird thing is, I knew for a fact that night actually took place. I couldn't remember if the moon path and doorway were included or whether it was just part of the dream I had. When something like that happens, you just don't forget, but so much has happened in the last ten years that it could easily be my mind playing games. As I went to put the towels away, I came back to the couch and noticed my phone had a text message from a 305 number. As I opened the text... "What's good Croney. It's me, Bellamy?" My heart instantly pounded. "What the fuck"! I mean I just dreamt about this guy less than a week ago. We haven't spoken in over nine years and all of a sudden, he's on my phone! I stared at my phone like if it was stink. It was just all to unreal. Then my phone rang. I let it ring the first time, then felt a bit of relief when it finally stopped ringing. But then it rang again. I took a deep breath... fuck it!

Leslie: Hello

Bellamy: Yo! What up? How are you?

Leslie: I'm good. How are you?

Bellamy: I'm great! Damn its good to hear your voice. You moved on and forgot all about me. How's Moncho, I bet he's big now!

Leslie: Yeah, he is. He'll be 13 in November. How's your mom and dad?

Bellamy: Everyone is doing great! I have a daughter now.

Leslie: That's what's up... Congratulations!

Bellamy: Umm, you probably gonna think I'm crazy. Not sure if you remember that night at the beach some years back. I had a dream about it last week. I tried calling the number I had for you, but it didn't work, so I went to your pop's house, and he gave me the new number.

Leslie: Wait! That night at the beach I remember, but I thought I dreamt the rest of it. Did we actually walk on water or some shit?

Bellamy: That's what I'm calling to ask you. Hold up! You had the same dream too?

Leslie: Yes, last Wednesday.

Bellamy: Fuck! Me too!

Leslie: That dream, that night and you have been on my mind, like heavy!

Bellamy: Same... what do you think it means?

Leslie: Not sure.

Bellamy: My lunch break is almost up. I'm gonna call you once I get off work.

Leslie: That's actually not a good idea. My dude is kind of stupid and I don't feel like arguing about you.

Bellamy: Damn, it's like that?

Leslie: For now, it is.

Bellamy: Alright, let's do this... you got my number, I got yours. Hit me up when you can. We gotta figure this dream out. Peace Croney.

Leslie: Bye Bell

I knew the dream and Bellamy calling so close to one another meant something, but I didn't have time in my life to handle it. My boyfriend was such a draining individual, I now had two kids and my youngest was just diagnosed with Autism. All I wanted to do was finish school and get a house with a back yard for my kids. I just didn't have the energy to go dream hunting and making sense of signs.

Selu watched diligently over Giza who had transformed into a golden sequoia to preserve his strength. Then carefully ensured the transition of the Amore, Adunai and Inaru into the era of their final lifetime, she placed her attention briefly on over to the Elohii whom had been enslaved and made to work upon fields and mines of the planet ElohI.

They spent their days working in the mountains and mines of the different regions removing the gems and various elements Giza placed into ElohI for her stability. Selu did not know what Okotadi was up to exactly, but she knew it was of no good. With her newfound essence of revival and the changes happening throughout the timelines, Selu made the decision to reach out to Cocijo, who was once her equal. Once upon a day as he worked tirelessly in the Northern mines removing jade and turquoise gems, he felt her surge within his conscience. "Keep working, I will reach out tonight as you rest", she said unto him. Cocijo kept working as instructed. As the Eliite patrol walked by, none were even aware that Selu attempted to commune with him. Later that evening after the Elohii retired to their dwellings, Cocijo found a quiet place to connect with Selu. As he focused his essence...

Cocijo: My heart, I thought I'd lost you

Selu: Our master Giza is merciful, He instructed me in the ways of self-sacrifice and honor. I am no longer your pair in form, but always in spirit. I am now goddess of resurrection and made watcher of Giza, the Elohii lineage, Adunai and Inaru. We have been given a chance to weaken Okotadi and the Destruction but, I fear, that I will need help. Giza, our lord, is very weak, he is very vulnerable. While I stand here with him and keep watch, I will need you.

Cocijo: What are my instructions?

Selu: It is a risk, but you must commune with the other Orishas

Cocijo: Ogun has taken a vow of silence ever since Okotadi emptied Oko of his purpose. He has fallen into despair.

Selu: Perhaps, we can give him life. Reach out to him and the others, undetected of course and share with them. As you rest tonight, I will connect you to the Amore.

Cocijo: Then I must not waste another moment. Honor and order!

Cocijo and Selu connected within the depths of his mind. He embraced her deeply. As she placed her forehead next to his she had shown him the memories from the Amore and even her last moments when Okotadi removed her crown. Once updated, Cocijo awakened empowered. Although his connection to Selu was beyond his physical form, it was enough to make him whole. Cocijo attempted to remain as neutral as possible, however Atticus detected a surge in energy. He did not know from where but needed to figure it out. As Cocijo inched his way next to Ogun, Ogun sensed Cocijo's aura. Ogun has finally spoken his first words after centuries of losing Oko.

Ogun: Is it Giza?

Cocijo placed his palm with Ogun's. He shared the memories Selu has given unto him. As Cocijo moved back to his side of the mine, Ogun, walked past Keui-Shen, touched palms with him and passed on Selu's memories. As Keui-Shen became excited, Ogun informed him to remain calm and continue working. "We must share with everyone, but undetected". Keui-Shen nodded and held on to the palms of every Elohii in his proximity. As the days passed Atticus felt a presence that he could not detect the source. He explained this to Adam. Adam then asked that all Orisha male and Elohii male types stop working and line up. The female type stopped to see what was taking place. As the men scurried to line up, Ogun stood next to Yemaya, and signaled that she gets next him. "What is it?" Ogun, with no time to explain for he knew if he took too long Atticus and Adam would detect his aura. He grabbed her palm and shared Selu's memories. Then he lined up with all the other male types. Yemaya smirked and grabbed her fellow Elohii female types touching not just their palms but exerting Selu's memories unto them as quickly as possible by placing her palms on their foreheads. As the female types became aware of Giza and Selu's plan, they remained as neutral as possible as to not tip the Eliites of their newfound information. As Selu watched from a distance, she noticed that her idea to empower the Elohii, rejuvenated Giza, but just minimally. His form sprouted new branches, blossoming indigo plum flora. Although it was not enough to fully generate him, it was a start. However, Selu could indicate the change in his breathing. It was stronger and more stable. Atticus was now confused as he could sense the energy among all of the Orisha. He even noticed how they all carried themselves differently. Instead of him and Adam dealing with it, they reached out to Okotadi.

Atticus: My lord, there has been a change. We believe the Elohii have been in communication with Giza.

Okotadi: Is that so? ... I knew that coward would not face me but try to sneak about... spreading his lies. Never mind that, let them enjoy. Let them celebrate! As a matter of fact, they may take the rest of the day off. They can resume working tomorrow. Feed them well... allow them to be content. They have been through much; they could use this extra support. Then tomorrow they will work more diligently believing in whatever hype Giza has sent unto them.

Atticus: Are you sure my lord? This could give them the opportunity to communicate with one another, giving them a chance to strategize against you.

Okotadi: Precisely! Then they will share this information with us.

Adam: Cunning... as you wish.

Adam lined up all Orisha and Elohii...

Adam: Okotadi our magnificent lord... has given you the remainder of the day. You will resume work in the morning. There has been a feast in honor of our lord in the main sanctuary... enjoy!

The Orisha and Elohii looked upon themselves in confusion, knowing that Okotadi was up to no good. As the Elohii met in the sanctuary they did their best not to mention or even think of the memory, so they carried on as usual. Selu now had access to all the Elohii and could tap into their conscience as needed. She knew that this was a risk as Okotadi could use it against them, but she also knew that he had no knowledge of self-sacrifice. If he were to empty them as he had done with Oko and herself, then she could retrieve them.

16. Engage

Although, I didn't want to, I watched the footage of how police officers Trotter and Cesar, approached Pearson with extreme prejudice and executed him in broad day. As the young man walked over to his car, they instantly attacked him without so much as to apprehend him then take him down for questioning. They cuffed him, slammed him to the ground bringing him to tears upon impact. They pressed their knees and elbows into his body, but not before offering his young body blows from their baton. They didn't sit him up, knowing well enough that the Miami sun had the sidewalk extremely hot. According to the looks on the officers' faces, they took pleasure enacting harm and disrespect on this young black body as his mother and community watched helplessly. I could see from their greyish colored auras that they were, Eliites, descendants from the Destruction and therefore, they lusted after killing Elohii. After watching the video five time straight on Instagram, I decided that was enough. Watching it once was already so traumatic. And although there was no evidence that Pearson was the right suspect, even if I searched for those who did commit a series of home invasions and armed robberies to remove the blame against Pearson, there would just be a different person of color dead instead of Pearson and that would not change anything. In fact, it would maintain the cycle and the preexisting history.

About a normal two weeks passed when my father called to tell me… "I know y'all don't watch the news, but you know the officers who killed that Antwan boy… they were acquitted". I couldn't believe what he was telling me, but at the same time, I wasn't even surprised. I shook my head in disbelief and disappointment, but to provide a response cause my dad couldn't see the gesture… "are you serious?" It's no secret the injustices and brutalities performed across our nations, our countries and around the world. Bodies with so much as a natural tan to complexions of much darker hues have suffered at the hands of those without. I thought about what my father said days after we'd spoken. Since I make it a personal habit to not watch the news or engage in worldly gossip, my father operates as my advisor to this world whether I want the information or not. Often times, I don't want to know about what unfairness the Eliites done cooked up. The lack of accountability by officers, political and religious officials is sickening, not to mention their blatant lack of morality. I just can't sit around waiting for an anchorperson to inform me of yet another unfortunate tragedy. To hear of another person, robbed of their life. A mother and father robbed of their child, or a child taken from their family and friends. It's disgusting…. the history, the legacy, and the damage that the Destruction have imposed upon humanity. These first children of the corrupted Origen, the descendants of Adam and Eve; Malice, Mentira, Atticus, Psyche and their Eliite progeny have polluted the world with prejudice and seditious intentions. Although Selu was able to retrieve some information about Okotadi's whereabouts, he was just too strong to dismantle. When the Eliites were bred and the Elohii enslaved, Okotadi's power amplified while Giza's minimized, along with that of his descendants. As I sat there with my mind moving between the young man Antwan and the officers not held responsible for his death; superiority versus slavery and Okotadi versus Giza, I knew there was some connection… but what? "If one moment could have such a grave effect upon the future of so many, what would it take to undo the effect? What was needed to evoke necessary change?" I wrestled with this paradox. "Okotadi is the god of logic, but he lacks reason… although Anh Sang was his equal, they never got a chance to create heirs. I wonder if that, at any time was a possibility. It probably doesn't even matter, we're here now and I don't know what to do. All I'm ever told is to look within or search my truth or get balanced… but how is any of that gonna help?" I had more questions than solutions. Why were the just, the honorable, the innocent persecuted? All these damn religions and world leaders and laws and yet people still suffer. They go hungry and cold. Children are abandoned and abused… This made absolutely no sense to me. How do we change the narrative? How do I fix anything? How do I handle this? "It would be cool if it didn't even happen" … and just like that, I had an idea! "What if the young man didn't lose his life… I mean he does, but we undo it… and undo it before the world? Like on social media and shit! In real time… now that, would have a great impact upon history! It should definitely punch Okotadi in his godlike nuts"! Elegua relished in my thought process, "now you're thinking like a prophet… it is your job to enact on behalf of society when leaders and the religions are no longer effective. Show the world the true power of Giza, the true power of the Amore… show yourself why you, are here! Your real purpose on Earth is to become more of who you really are. To live to the highest degree of what is pure, what is honest, what is natural and what feels like the real you." I was so excited that I finally had a plan to "maybe" cause a form of change. Attempting to resurrect Pearson seemed like the best course of action and to do it in front of the fucking police was gonna be so damn satisfying!!!

But first things first. I needed to formally meet the goddess who's will I embodied.

As I assured myself that this was the plan, I now needed to meet Inaru. I googled how to perform a séance, but the stuff that populated was too weird and I definitely didn't know where to find a goat this time of night. Then, "just look within" in a voice that was not mine or

E's gently instructed me. I went into my bathroom, stared at myself in the mirror, gripped the edge of the sink with a certain level of anxiety. I looked at myself… "it's going to be fine" … then once I had calmed my breathing… I loosened my grip, closed my eyes and a few moments later, opened them to find someone other than myself staring back. "Free-key" … I raised my right hand as did the image in the mirror. I looked to my left as did the image in the mirror. I smiled as did the image in the mirror. I then took a huge breath… "hello", the image in the mirror smiled and spoke… "finally! Leslie I am pleased to officially meet you. I've waited for this moment for quite some time. Given the hostilities of this realm, I am honored to have embodied such a gentle essence."

Leslie: I'm not sure what to say. But now that I'm looking at you, I've dreamt about you so many times.

Inaru: When my noble and great father Giza placed Adunai and I into the maternal grace of the Amore, my essence was still. While I did not know what was happening, I only hoped, well I trusted that I would encounter a worthy host. However, I did not know that I would be hidden within you for so long.

Leslie: How long have you been with or inside of me? … that is the oddest question I've ever asked.

Inaru: Your lineage is attached to mine, but my will entered your essence the night you and Bellamy stepped directly into the Amore.

Leslie: Wait! So that part of the night actually happened? Damn, you've been in there a good while… Also, I'm sorry for being a goober.

Inaru: Yes, your innocence and personality is most amusing, but I appreciate the honest and pure soul that you are.

Leslie: So now what?

Inaru: Your idea to resurrect the young man is valid. But we will need to do things in order. We must awaken Adunai. You are correct in your attraction and assumption of Bellamy. Adunai's will lives within him. I can sense it, but I notice that he is missing his link to the Amore.

Elegua: I may be of assistance. After your stillness and long after, I was made to keep Adunai's chakras so he would not be tracked once reborn. During our siege in Songhai, Malice and Psyche outwitted Adunai, bringing forth the fall of the empire. It was my sacrifice to die for you both, that Selu retrieved my essence. She made me watcher, a god of destiny and spiritual doorways and therefore I monitor the transition of Elohii, particularly prophets. I have been made guardian of your connective source. While I have the majority of his essence, you my dear have his heart. It was the piece of him that you needed so you could detect him… wherever you go.

Leslie: That's beautiful! And explains so much…This man is gonna think I'm insane when I tell him this.

Inaru: You mustn't tell him. But we will show him.

The following months, I went over and over what I would tell Bell once I had seen him. He told me to hit him up once my life regulated, but I didn't think, nor did he probably expect that would take years. I just felt like too much time has passed on my end to pour my feelings out to him, let alone tell him that we are somehow fated to stop a god from destroying the world. I was officially down in Miami for the summer and knew the time was now or never. I took a deep breath and texted Bellamy. "Hey, how's it going? I'm down here for a few weeks and wanted to know if you'd like to meet up?" He instantly replied, "Absolutely. I hit you up a while back tho. I guess you weren't kidding, that nigga had you on lock, lol." Although he was teasing, I had been through what I considered an extremely traumatic relationship, not just for me but for my sons, especially my eldest. After a few minutes since I hadn't said anything, he hit me with, "you at your pops? I can pull up about 7pm." I told him that would work. After that I exhaled deeply but my nerves were still on the fritz, so I thought that I'd have a blunt and yoga session about 5pm, then shower and get ready for him. As I placed my mat on the back porch, put my "Releasing Fear (Solfeggio 396 Hz)" meditating frequency, and eased my way onto the mat, it hadn't even been three minutes before I slid into a deep state. I instantly found myself back in my car on Capital Circle N.E. as people left their cars in the middle of the streets and ran in terror. As I stood out of my car, I remembered being in this dream already. I pinched my arm, which I could feel, but knew that this was all wrong. My body was in Miami, on my dad's back porch. How did I end up here? This already happened! As I exited my car, the sky was clearly angry. The clouds were in those weird hand gestures. The wind was aggressive; lightning and thunder was making a lot of noise; except this time I was not lured out of the chaos but put into it. The hand shaped clouds began to animate. They started spinning around, slowly at first then as the minutes passed, they spiraled more intensely. Then the wind spiked as the clouds spun even more rapidly, spinning into a vortex. When I saw the clouds spin out of the sky and into a tornado, I understood why everyone was leaving their cars and running, so I decided to do the same thing except for my body would not let me. I could move towards the tornado of doom, but could not retreat, "ain't this bout a bitch!... um hello, Elegua, Ogun... Oya! Someone"!!! No one answered. "Ok, think", then I remembered in this moment, that I had just purchased Makaveli, but after exiting my car I was only able to move forward. I struggled with myself to move to the right but could not and every step forward was a step that I could not return. My heart started pounding and I was freaking out. And if things could not get worst, they did! Once the tornado stopped a large and I mean large being stood out of the tornado. She had to be over a hundred feet tall. "Ok, ok...so I'm gonna die! This is the moment I die! Aye...

Oya, Elegua...shit Jehovah! Mufasa! Any fucking body!!! Please!" No one answered, no one showed up, there was me, everybody who was running away and now this big ass woman thing. After this being emerged, and because obviously I couldn't stop glowing, she spotted me without hesitation. As she positioned her body facing mine, the center of her body had the same tornado type spin, then Malice jumped from it. I remember him from viewing the beginning. Not only did he come out of this belly portal, but so did Mentira and thirty to fifty of their Eliite army. I was so, fucking scared! So naturally, I started laughing hysterically. This was the most insane stupidest shit ever, I couldn't run, I couldn't get my gun, I didn't know how to exit my conscience... I was basically dead. "Trust what lives in you" I heard these words clear as day, but there was no one on my team. "Hey, where y'all at?", but I got no instruction other than this. "Ok, trust, trust, trust.... (exhale) trust, trust, trust... trust, ooohhhh trust" ... I couldn't do anything but repeat these words. Then as I looked down, I noticed my root and sacral chakra were lit. As I turned my head and caught a glimpse of my reflection in my car, I noticed all of my chakras were lit except for my crown. I thought for a second and then remembered that Elegua removed it. How could I be fully functional and not have all my chakras, is what I thought. Since this thought naturally occurred, maybe this was the moment that I was waiting on... I mean Elegua did tell me to trust what was in me and what was in me was fear that led me to thinking that I needed my crown... good answer, good answer! So, I took a chance and placed my mind to the very moment where he reached for it. Although I could not exit to where I initially was, this moment seemed to open without any issues. As Elegua stepped forward to remove my crown, I caught his hand. I had stopped him from removing it and as I opened my eyes I looked over at my reflection and saw that my crown chakra was lit. I thought this must mean something, so I prepared my mind. "Ok, its just me...body, chakras, spirit, I need us to all act as one. I need protection, I need gear", the moment I connected with myself and trusted in my lights to give me what I needed... I suddenly had golden and jeweled armor. "Oh yea baby!" I was so stoked, "Ok, Ok... I need weapons", I was provided with daggers, couple of spears and a golden chopper. "Last but not least, I need a defensive aura", the crown chakra concealed me within the glow of the Amore, and although I had no person with me, I remembered that I had all my ancestral essence with me... "What ya'll waiting on, I been ready", I took my chopper and started to take out as many of the Eliites as possible. Straight head shots might I add... "damn, I hope somebody was recording this"! I took one of my three spears and aimed them straight at Malice. I did not want to engage with him or any of his four arms in a fist fight. As I aimed my first spear, he caught it with ease. I did become intimidated, so I threw all of my spears at him, and as he held on to all three, the last two piercing straight threw his palms, I commanded that they grapple and hook into the ground. This pinned him, now it was Mentira and Eliites to deal with. I moved one step closer, but not without executing many more of their army. Mentira, I did not know what her powers were, but I tried my best to not let them get close enough to touch me. My suit clearly had a mind of its own, as jade and iron star shaped blades were lined up for the throwing… so I threw them at her… and did I mention, the accuracy! As they sliced her form and pushed her back, I noticed that the very large form was affected with every slice I gave Mentira. Right away I knew they were linked. She must be an illusionist of some kind. I spoke to myself, "It would be nice, if I could grow as big as her". Moments later I was staring at Mentira's enlarged form at eye's view. I stepped on so many Eliites as I made my way closer. But I got too cocky with my powers that I didn't stop to think, how am I winning and why haven't they blitzed yet?

By the time I realized this there was a hand reaching out of the portal before me "o, right… this is a trap." The hand that extended out of the form locked onto my solar plexus chakra and pulled me inside. As my body entered what appeared to be the absence of light and sound from the beginning, there was a small opening towards the opposite end where the hand was guiding me. Once arrived, I was standing there before Okotadi. As I entered his realm, I told my form to keep a

dagger in hand. "Welcome. Although I do not recognize your form…
it is your will, your essence I would know anywhere Inaru, your
grace." He kneeled before me, then stood up with an eager and
pleasantly sinister look on his face. His skin was pale, and much of it
was covered in scattered scales, burns, keloids, and scars. He wore a
black robe which was not closed and pants whose hems were
distressed and worn out as if these were the only pair he owned. I
couldn't see his feet, just his toes which had raptor like talons. As I
glanced around it was clear to see that I was in his atmosphere on
Origen. I stood there silently, eyes locked onto him and every move
he made, he insisted with a monologue…

Okotadi: I've been waiting for you. I must admit my brother has truly
enhanced his technique. His strategy during our earlier existence, was
never this impressive, but recently his methods have changed. He's
evolved and now, a worthy opponent. See, you can't properly grow,
without facing adversity. But I see now that he wants my logic, my
power for himself that he's even willing to sacrifice his own heirs for
it. I have known you Leslie, for a short while now, and you seem to be
a pretty easy-going person. I would never waste the lives of my
descendants… oh, but brother… thinks he can just waste the lives of
so many innocents and that there will be no consequences. Tell me
Leslie, did my brother tell you that you are doing something noble?
Hmm, did he say that you would be doing a great and noble DEED by

sacrificing your life and the lives of everyone you hold dear? He's a trickster, a liar and in the game of it all…a LOSER (chuckling).

As Okotadi spoke he got closer. He was clearly deranged and unstable. As he stood in my face, his serpent tongue licked his lips, but I knew that if he so much as moved any closer, I was ready to fuck him up! "What did he promise you… huh, fame, glory, riches… immor..tal..ity? … all which I can make come true" … then he did it… he came closer and that's when I sliced his neck then plunged my dagger deep into it. Okotadi stumbled back, placed his hand on the dagger and felt around the opening I'd created across his throat and began to laugh hysterically. "Oh, my dear, you thought… you thought you could hurt me? No, no no no…because you possess the will of Inaru, my beloved. I cannot hurt you, nor would I, you are my family… but you are in my realm. I have catalysts and algorithms everywhere, no one can hurt me here… not even I can cause myself harm. I've contemplated on ways to just end it all, but then when I fail, as I have many times over, I just think of new ways to defeat my brother in this ever-lasting game, we've played since our beginning". Okotadi removed the dagger from his neck, which drew not even a spot of blood and politely reversed the handle and handed it back. He took his scaly hand, touched the slice on his neck, which immediately disappeared. "You go on now Leslie, I simply wanted you to meet me directly so you could make the decision to continue with your mission for… yourself. Have you even met my brother? The so-called Giza, the Great, that you are willing to sacrifice it all for?" He bowed, then sent me back… As my breath, soul and body all attached I was once again on my dad's back porch. My alarm rang, but I didn't dismiss nor snooze it, all I could think was how I fucked up. The only reason he knew me was because I put the crown chakra back, I undid what Elegua did for my protection. I tried to reach out to him or connect to anyone at this point but failed. I think by me stopping Elegua I may have put us all at jeopardy and given Okotadi, the upper hand. As I sat there a few more minutes, I picked up my phone and realized that it was 6:50pm. I showered and got dressed really quickly, but by 7:20pm, Bellamy had not reached out nor was he here. One thing about Bell, no matter how much time has passed, if he said he was coming and at a specific time, this is something you could always count on. I called him and texted him, but no reply. I was starting to panic, I think, I just fucked it all up and not just for myself but for my family, for Bellamy, for Giza and maybe all of humanity.

17. Intersect

"I Leslie Croney am the eldest daughter of a lineage of eldest daughters that descends from thee eldest daughter Inaru; heiress to the Creators of Origen and queen mother of all Elohii people. I descend from the first matriarch of the divine, queens, sisters, warriors, and survivors from the Battle of First. I am heir to women that have lived, died and were reborn into the divine right of Elohii prophets and guardians of the lineage. After Selu was promoted to goddess of Resurrection, she and Giza established the Rites of Elders, granting allegiance to eldest daughters of any Orisha lineage to house the will of Inaru; the first daughter… until the Destruction and Okotadi himself have been weakened. I Leslie Croney, have been sworn to carry out the Awakening; the final decree issued to Elohii prophets. Only thing is… I really don't know what the fuck I'm doing!". The closer I got to the end of what I thought would be my final chapter, the story seemed to take on a life of its own. I sat to my desk a few minutes longer and decided to save what I had written, because I didn't want to force a story but rather allow it to flow from me freely.

The very next morning as I prepared for the day, I dropped my son off to school and headed to work. As I stopped to the light at the intersection of Tennessee St. and Macomb, I saw a cloud in the sky to my right that looked like a palm. I stared at it, then ignored it as soon as the light turned green and made my way to campus. As I parked in the faculty parking at Florida State across from Diffenbaugh, I exited my car and noticed the exact same cloud, but it was now to my left. As I strapped on my bags and grabbed my things to head towards my building, I did so in complete distraction of the cloud. There was something vaguely familiar about it. I know that I had just written fifteen chapters in my book, but to see a cloud shaped like the palm of a hand just as I had written about, was a little eerie. I double checked that I had everything to start my day, locked my car, dropped my keys in my bag, crossed the street, got in the elevator, hit the 4th floor button, and let out a deep sigh... I was ready for this Monday morning. As I stepped out onto what I thought was the 4th floor, nothing looked familiar. The offices that are normally to my right and my office door on the left, were not there. I attempted to double check the floor number that's usually on the corner of the elevator but as I turned around, there was no elevator... in fact, there was nothing. I stood there looking ever so slowly at this place that I did not recognize. I turned around several times as if that was supposed to do something until, I mouthed, "just stop... and let's think". I had not done anything out of the ordinary nor was I at my desk writing my story. I took a step down this corridor which seemed to go on and on. I finally reached a door to my left. Although I was apprehensive in opening it, this was the only door in sight, so my options to do something…hell anything… were pretty slim. I took a deep breath, then twisted the doorknob. I entered just slightly, peeking a portion of my body through, just in case. But of course, once I peeked in, the door behind me had now evaporated and it was just me standing there… peeking. Oh, how I thought this was such bullshit. I pinched my arm to see what was really happening and as luck would have it, I felt it. "Ok, so we're back to this", as I stated as much the word "this" echoed and the sound ricocheted down this long new hallway… but this time at the very end, there was the golden shimmery eye again. I had to be dead, this was the only thing that made sense. Maybe as I exited my car a random bullet took my life and now, I was in some sort of afterlife. There is no way that the story I had been writing on for years could actually be real. I pinched myself again just to make sure and yep, I could still feel it. I put my work bags and my tumbler filled with an oatmeal banana smoothie down on the floor, slid my phone into my back pocket and walked carefully down the hallway. With every step I took random glowing lights, each a color of the spectrum began to appear on both sides of the hallway. As I reached the eye, I became nervous. There was no one here except me, those sphere-like bright lights and this eye. I stared at the eye for a few minutes. I even stuck my hand through it a few times, which did absolutely nothing. I stepped around it, to see what was behind it, but when I did the eye was not there. I stepped back around it was there, I stepped behind again, not there. I wasn't gonna keep doing this just in case someone was watching so I sat down in criss cross applesauce before the eye. "Ok, think... how could this be happening? I thought this was just my imagination... running away with me, it was just my imagination... running, away from me", as I sat there singing the words to the Temptations Imagination song, I could not help but get into it... "every night on my knees I pray, dear lord... hear my plead... don't ever let another take her love from me, or I would surely die" ... I really thought to myself that if someone were watching this that they would assume I was crazy and let me leave, but if I was dead then at least I had a sense of peace about it. Suddenly a familiar voice, "I can assure you that you are not dead, but you are off pitch", I stood up ever so quickly and embraced Elegua with such joy!

Leslie: Dude! So this, is real? Although I've been writing this story, part of me knew it was familiar...

Elegua: After you planted the crown chakra, you exposed yourself, but you also exposed Okotadi. We have not been able to catch a glimpse of his realm as to assess for the algorithms that protect it.

Leslie: Wait... you used me?

Elegua: We knew that you would place the gem back and therefore used the opportunity along with your memory of his realm to produce catalysts that may serve to weaken his barrier.

Leslie: Oh

Elegua: Selu, thought it best to undo what you've learned but leave you with just enough insight about what had actually taken place. But it seems that your opportunistic behavior decided to turn your private thoughts into a novel.

Leslie: Well… they are my thoughts… and I thought it would make an interesting book. And how was I supposed to know that I couldn't use it to try and make money. So, what happens now?

Elegua: You awaken

As I opened my eyes, I was laying on my couch, in my own apartment. I sat up and glanced at the time, 4:07 am I went to the bathroom and as I sat there peeing, I quietly hummed Imagination to myself. As I washed my hands and took a quick look at myself in the mirror, I noticed my tattoos were back… which meant that I was not nuts, but a beacon to house the will of a goddess. I took my phone and read through different notes I had in my Memo along with the daily text messages of family and friends. I reacquainted my past self with my current life. In doing this it all started to come back to me. About 7 am as I read the last note in my phone a text message from Bellamy came through. QOTD: "Confrontation and resolution are not only requisites but necessities to evoke change, to evoke growth, and eventually, to evoke peace". I was happy to see that he was fine and that my impulsive behavior had not placed him in danger. I replied "deep" and added the Black power fist emoji.

18. Awakening

Okotadi paced about for weeks contemplating his possible course of actions. "So, Leslie is the paragon with which he will attempt to defeat me, but I now know who she is. But where has he placed Adunai? If Malice dismantled him and Inaru both, during their reign in Sahel, how is it that she is now here?" Okotadi, continued thinking aloud about the information he'd currently absorbed. "Giza must be repurposing their essence, but how? His grasp on the Elohii and our All, must tax his strength... could he possibly be much stronger than I anticipated? No...no... he would've attempted to defeat me head on... what if it is not him? It could not be Adunai, although it would explain his absence, he is bound by limitations. Who offers Giza aid? Who could possess such power? Pisim is weakened and Anh Sang is broken?" Okotadi thought that he was generous enough and that it was time for the Orisha and Elohii to provide him with the missing pieces.

Okotadi: Gather around, gather around. It is now time for a little story. I know that Giza has been in communication with you. He has inspired you all and it is now time that you inspire me. So, who will be the first among you to share... Come now, no need to be shy...

The Elohii stood in total silence, indicating not even the slightest hint of the memories they'd been given.

Atticus: Perhaps, some persuasion my lord.

Okotadi: Yes Atticus. Bring the younglings forth.

As the Eliites brought forth the progeny of the Elohii, the elder Elohii and Orishas did not flinch, for they were instructed by Selu that the persecution of any Elohii, by the hands of the Destruction would be repurposed for Giza and infused with the Amore. As the younglings stood before Okotadi, they too were instructed in the ways of Honor and Order. All Elohii from birth were taught to trust in the will of their Creator Giza, in the will of the All. As Okotadi stood, he stalked slowly about each of the progeny, hoping to evoke fear. But he soon became agitated that even the children were resilient. "Enough! You… step forward." As Oko's eldest son Chango stepped forward as instructed, he did so with honor and strength. Chango's eyes were locked onto Okotadi's. There was not so much as a change in his breathing. "Yes, you reek of your father's scent and arrogance. A trait inherited from your Creator of Origen no doubt. You will meet the same fate as your father, but I will not drain you of your essence. Rather, you will serve as an example to the others of what happens when you defy your lord. Malice if you could, please… execute with extreme prejudice." As Malice approached Chango, the ground trembled with every step he took, but this did not weaken Chango's heart. As Malice attempted to reach the young Elohii, Chango swiftly rolled out of Malice's way then reached into the sky retrieving lightning rods. Then he stood in his fighting stance. Electricity bolted through his eyes and form, "I will not stand idle, I will not make it easy for you!" Malice grinned, then leaped into the air, and came crashing down. His sheer weight made the ground beneath Chango collapse, but this did not alter the young man's disposition. When the ground settled Chango threw his lightning bolts at Malice, then clapped his thundering hands at him, knocking Malice backwards. Okotadi stood there watching as his order for Malice to execute the young Elohii had been defied by Chango's retaliation. After Malice stumbled back just slightly, Chango aimed and threw lightning rods at Okotadi, one of the rods grazed Okotadi on the arm. The Orisha and Elohii were ready to pursue Okotadi, but Selu tapped into them, "please allow it to happen. If there is a chance for us to weaken Okotadi, a sacrifice must be made." Although many of the Elohii were ready to fight and die alongside Chango, they knew they needed to trust in Selu, which meant trusting in Giza. Okotadi infuriated, extended his hand which drew Chango's form directly into Malice's left arms. Ogun took a step forward, followed by the other Orisha and Elohii, they all bent the knee, placing their palms onto their crowns and in unisons, "May the energy that sustains you, never rest and forever reign." Malice constricted Chango's form until the electricity that ran through it, shorted. Chango began to struggle and gasp for air. When Malice released him, the youngling was weakened as he had been crushed by Malice's four powerful arms, like a raptorboa on the kill of his prey. Chango gathered the strength he had left and attempted to stand, but the ivory bones in his form had been severely crushed. Still, the youngling, squirmed, inching himself toward Malice with the determination to continue his fight. Malice balled up his four fists and began pounding… and pounding… and pounding… and pounding upon Chango's form, until the progeny inched no more. Essence seeped from his mouth and ears and onto the grounds of ElohI. Okotadi turned to see the expression on the faces of the Elohii, many were shocked to see their brother dead. Many were sad, but they all were enraged. As they all stayed there kneeling, Chango's younger brother, who now became the eldest, Elegua stood, walked over to his brother's lifeless body, took off his robe and placed it over him. "You are now with our supreme lord, he will guarantee you safe passage brother, until we meet again. Honor and order."

At the moment of Chango's death Selu placed his potential within the Amore. She preserved his will for the precise moment where he could live once more. The Elohii, did not make a sound, as they all vowed silence in respect of their beloved Chango. Okotadi perplexed, did not order the Elohii to return to their quarters, he knew well enough to allow them to mourn. As the male types collected Chango's form, they gathered in the West to place him beneath the Baobab graves where those who perished during the Battle of the First laid in peace.

The summer heat along with the riots across the country continued. While the officers in the execution of Antwan Pearson were exonerated, the nation and many parts of the world were in an uproar. Although I did not want to be down here, I needed to finally meet up with Bellamy. The last time I tried, Okotadi engaged because of my foolishness but this time I was ready, and nothing was going to get in our way. Now that Inaru and I know that Bellamy houses the will of Adunai, it is up to us and Elegua to import Adunai's chakras into him so they can become one. Once we do this, then we can attempt to resurrect Pearson before the world. Hopefully this will be enough to help Giza. While this sounds pretty straight forward, after Adunai has been awakened Okotadi will know where he is and once, we awaken Pearson, Okotadi would have pieced everything all together and there's no telling what he and the Destruction will do. I texted Bellamy to meet me at Hallandale beach lifeguard tower #9 about 8pm. He responded "sentimental… I'll be there." As I sat nervously in my car, I remembered that I had half a blunt in my bag. Once I lit it up and dragged on it maybe four times, Bell pulled up. He tapped on my window and shook his head. "You know smoking is no good for you?". I blew the smoke out slowly, then gestured the blunt in his direction, "you may need to hit this, cause I gotta show you some shit... come on." As we made it to "our thrones", Bellamy had such a big smile on his face...

Leslie: Why are you smiling?

Bellamy: It's been decades since we been out here.

Leslie: I know... so what do you remember about the night we were last here?

Bellamy: I remember you took advantage of me. I also remember how big and full the moon was... I also think we was walking on water.

Leslie: Do you trust me?

Bellamy: Maybe

Leslie: I'm going to place my hand on your forehead and my other hand on mine. I need you to hold still, no matter what happens.

Bellamy: Alright

I took my sweater off. You could tell by Bellamy's facial expressions that he was a little weirded out, but much was expected as my tattoos were glowing along with all my chakras. I tried to place my palm on his forehead, but he slapped my hand down, "yo Croney, what the fuck?" I took a deep breath...

Leslie: I know this is weird, but the only way I can tell you what's going on and what has to happen is by showing you. Please, Bell... just trust me. I would never let anything happen to you... ok. Take a deep breath.

Bellamy: If I die, I'm killing you!

Leslie: I wouldn't expect anything less.

Bellamy took a big breath, stepped closer and then I carefully placed my palm on my crown, then on his. I channeled the memories of what I had learned from the Amore, to catch him up to speed. As we both entered a fifth level of consciousness, Inaru and Elegua were there to greet us.

Inaru: Welcome

Bellamy: Who the fuck are you! Yo Croney are we in your mind?

Leslie: Relax B... we are, but we are also in yours as well. We are in a fifth level, which is a space that we can connect with other minds, so to speak. You are going to get a crash course in the Beginning.

Elegua: But first thing first my king. Here you are

Elegua held out a small drawstring bag similar to the one he placed the lavender quartz he removed from me. As he took Bellamy's hand, he spoke the decree of the Awakening onto him, then placed his chakras into his form.

Bellamy: Wait... my king? I'm a king? Like T'Challa?

Leslie: Something like that.

As Elegua placed Adunai's essence into Bellamy's form, instantly Adunai appeared. He and Inaru embraced, and made out a bit, then introduced himself.

Inaru: We haven't much time. Adunai, I have been intersected with Leslie as you have now intersected with Bellamy, they house our will in this lifetime. We have found a way that may weaken Okotadi, but it will take all of us to do so.

Leslie extracted Adunai's heart chakra from her form, then placed it into Bellamy's palm. "This is what drew me to you instantly"

Adunai: I gave this to you Inaru before we were made to lay still.

Inaru: It is the reason why we are here. It was Leslie's strong love for Bellamy and my connection to you that made our meet possible.

Bellamy: Wait, Les… you love me, love me?

Leslie: Since the moment I laid eyes on you.

Inaru: It is rare to find someone who aligns, but you two were the perfect pairing. We salute you!

Elegua: I do not mean to break up this bond, but once we break Okotadi would have sensed this. If we are going to change history, we must do so now.

As I removed my palms from my and Bellamy's crown, he stood there looking at me with a big smile.

Leslie: Are you intact?

Bellamy: We are

Leslie: Do you know what we have to do?

Bellamy: Yes!

Just as Bell responded the moonlight shun across the ocean, just like that night twenty years ago. I looked over at Bell and he at me, "we ride together, we die together", I laughed, "you are such a dork." As we made our way onto the lit path, we walked until we reached a door. As we entered, our destiny had now fallen into place. Elegua met us through the door, which led to a long hallway, with that same gold shimmery eye towards the end. "It is time", then gestured we walk on. Every step we took towards the eye a person on each side of the hallway turned from their watch, bent the knee, and placed their palm on their crown. As we got to the end, Bellamy whispered, "Aye is that DMX?" I looked over at him and shook my head yes excitedly, but did not utter a word, for I knew, whatever was going to happen next would be epic.

Leslie: We have to resurrect this young man before the world

Bellamy: Alright. How many resurrections have you performed?

Leslie: None

Bellamy: What?

Leslie: Well, I haven't exactly been through any of this before.

Bellamy: Are we going to die?

Leslie: Nah!... I mean maybe. I don't really fucking know!

Bellamy: Yo Croney, I got kids, I got a job...damn

Leslie: I know! So do I! But I don't think we can back away from this.

Elegua: You both are here because it is your right as well as your duty. You both are fated in this time. You have been ordained by the supreme source. You both house the essence that allows for the will of our king father and queen mother. You are equals and the only two that can undo the chaos which has been unleashed. Trust in what lives within. It will guide you both. Honor and order!

I took Bell by the hand, "I won't let anything happen to you. I got you Bell! In this life and every other life." Bellamy then placed his hand over mine, "I know you do, and for what it's worth, I damn sure love you too! Always have and always will." We both took deep breaths, then walked through the eye. Both Bellamy and I were thrusted through the Amore. Until now the things that have happened to me have happened spiritually, particularly to keep things silenced from Okotadi and his Destruction, but now, we were about to exit the Amore. This portal has been the thing keeping us safe. And now that we exit it, we will be in real time as well as rare form. We reached what appeared to be the edge of the eye for we could see people on the other end.

Anchorwoman Henry: We've been here at the scene waiting, one moment (holding her ear receiving confirmation) … yes it has just been announced. The young man, Antwan Pearson has been reported deceased. After receiving severe and fatal blows from officers Trotter and Cesar while in handcuffs. As you can see behind me his body is still present on scene, where medical examiners have concluded that Pearson was definitely a victim of what can be described as brutal and blunt force trauma. Time of death has been declared, however is not being released at this moment as this is now said to be an ongoing investigation. Carol City Chief of Police Ruiz along with city officials have announced that the officers involved will not be available for questioning and that the department will offer an official statement once the scene has been cleared. Carol City, the greater Miami and Broward areas and citizens around the world are outraged! Over what is now the loss of yet another young black man by law enforcement. What in the world!... Wait... There appears to be... is that a fucking eye!? Don are you getting this!?

Don: Hell yeah, I'm getting this shit! And that's a big ass eye!

The golden shimmery eye portal appeared on the intersection of 183rd and 27th in the plaza behind the McDonald's. Everyone was in a panic, running, and screaming away from the light. Many exited and abandoned their cars while others jumped into the abandoned cars trying to escape this unknown floating eye. Right before Bellamy and I exited, Elegua, handed Bellamy a lavender quartz stone, "place this into Pearson's crown." Then he handed me a jade malachite stone, "place this into Pearson's heart. Place your palms onto your crown and your heart, then speak the words of Origen."

As we exited the eye, we noticed that we looked like ourselves, but not really. Words from the decree covered our entire form, so much so that we did not have on any clothes but were not naked. The glow from our chakras were on full display and that light shielded us. We spotted Pearson laying upon the ground, lifeless and started to walk towards the young man. Police officers that had set up barricades to enforce citizens to remain behind had now turned and aimed their weapons in our direction.

Bellamy: We should scare them

Leslie: Stay focused

News crews recorded our entrance into the city, while many people had their phones out recording us as well. Police officers opened fire, the bullets did not harm us.

Bellamy: Fucking cool... were indestructible baby!

Leslie: Damn straight, I think we should scare them just for shooting at us

Bellamy: Now you talking!

Bellamy picked up two police vehicles and threw them towards the open avenue, "roooooaarrr bitches." Many of the officers that had opened fire ran in fear of us. I laughed so hard but remembered the last time I was given power and got cocky that I also messed things up. "Hey, that's enough, we have a job to do." As we finally reached Pearson's body, Bellamy and I approached the medical examiners with a pleasant greeting. They backed up and allowed us to move towards Pearson's lifeless form. I placed the jade malachite into Pearson's heart, then placed my palm to my own heart. Bell then placed the lavender quartz in Pearson's crown as he placed his palm to his own crown. Together we recited, "May the energy that sustains you, never rest and forever reign." As we spoke these words nothing changed with Pearson's body. But the weather drastically settled, and the scene was now in complete silence. The people that had been running in fear and panic were now standing by and at our full attention. Even though we had not been loud in reciting the words of Origen, Bell looked around in amazement, "Yo Croney... you hearing this shit?" I was so focused on our mission that I hadn't even noticed, until he said it.

Family and friends of Pearson, as well as the community... even the news crew had started to recite in unison, "may the energy that sustains you, never rest and forever reign." These Elohii descendants who had forgotten over time of their natural essence were compelled by the vibe me, and Bellamy were exerting. And for the first time maybe since the beginning, everyone Elohii in proximity or in witness of the words of Origen had channeled in... as they continued reciting the language of Origen appeared across Pearson's form. His crown chakra illuminated then his heart chakra. Pearson opened his eyes, took a deep breath and stood up.

Don: (Watching through his live camera) God damn!... that boy alive!?
Anchorwoman Henry: Nigga, I hope you still rolling! (exhales, then composes herself) I cannot believe this! ... Pearson who was moments ago confirmed deceased has now risen in what appears to be some sort of alien resurrection.
As Pearson stood, his mother and brother ran into his arms. They could not believe that he was alive. "Oh, my lord, thank you Jesus or whoever you both are... this is such a miracle...O Twan", his mother cried tears of joy and excitement as she held onto her son. Pearson looked around at the community cheering and applauding in amazement. He then looked over at me and Bellamy, placing his fist upon his crown and everyone else did the same, as an expression of gratitude. We felt a strong sense of accomplishment as we executed what we aimed to do. Moments later a large meteor crashed down, smashing the Taco Bell into rubble.
Leslie: Shit!
Bellamy: What's happening?
Leslie: The Destruction is happening... All right people, run! Get away from here... Go!

Antwan: You heard, everybody take cover… Ma, I love you… now go! Get somewhere safe!

Bellamy: What do we do, can we take them?

Leslie: We ride together…

Bellamy: Bet

Leslie: Alright Inaru, I need all you can give me. I need you to be large and a bad bitch!

Inaru complied. My form elevated maybe three stories in height, I retracted claws and fangs. My body was covered in golden and jeweled armor, and I was fully equipped with weaponry. My eyes were locked onto Mentira. Bellamy's form grew to match Malice's stature and he even developed two more sets of arms. Adunai gave Bellamy iron and diamond spiked steel knuckles for all four hands, gear, and a sexy ass sword. And although we were not expecting it, Pearson was given by Selu, the potential of Chango. Pearson too, had a thunder bow and lightning arrows. His form had enlarged, and the Amore shielded his body as well. We had positioned ourselves but did not move until Malice and Mentira did. They stood there waiting, just then more meteors rained down as their outer shell crumbled upon impact, children of the Destruction, the Eliites poured out, fully decorated with weapons and armor. "I don't know if we're enough", Bellamy looked over at me, "We're enough!" Pearson ran before us, shooting his lightning rods into the air, electrocuting the many meteors that started to fall from the sky, killing Eliites on impact. Bellamy and I followed his lead, hurling daggers and shooting them from falling onto the ground, for we knew they were filled with more Eliites. The Eliites that survived began running in our direction, I took my golden chopper and John Wick shooting skills and started to take out as many of them as possible. I did not want them to cross 183rd street. Malice began to run in our direction; therefore, Bellamy began to run in his direction, just as they collided Bellamy uppercut Malice into the air. Mentira stood still, staring at me, then suddenly disappeared. She appeared near the McDonald's, then disappeared again and reappearing across the street near Checkers. I couldn't take my eyes off the Eliites as they ran in waves toward me and Pearson, but I had to be alert, because I knew she would try a sneak attack. All of a sudden it happened; she dug her dagger into my shoulder blade. Pearson thunder clapped at her, blowing her back, but the piercing pain placed a hinder in my shooting. The Eliites gained speed and covered ground quickly. I was able to reach behind me with my left arm and yanked the dagger out, then ran towards her and plunged it into her thigh, twisting it as I pushed it in deeper. I unleashed my claws upon her form. I slashed and sliced until there was not much space left on her form to lacerate. Many of the Eliites jumped onto me, stabbing, and biting at me. Bellamy and Malice continued to duke it out. Malice jumped into the air and came crashing down attempting to disorient the ground beneath Bellamy. But as Malice touched down, Bell picked up the M sign from McDonald's and homerunned Malice's ass back into the air, driving him higher and higher with every hit. When Bellamy touched down, he stomped upon many Eliites that attacked him. Then several minutes later after Mentira had been laid out, Malice's body came crashing down, placing a large crater into the middle of the street. Bellamy was able to subdue Malice especially since his equal had been weakened. Bellamy stood over Malice making sure he was unconscious, "you just got knocked the fuck out!" After what was a taxing battle between us and these anti-Elohii, Malice, Mentira, their bodies instantly vanished. Many of the citizens that hid nearby cheered and ran towards us. Bellamy, Pearson, and I stood there feeling proud at what we had done. Not only did we perform a successful resurrection but kicked the Destruction's ass.

Okotadi exploded! He was outraged that he did not predict this particular outcome, "BROTHER! BROTHER! You sneaky, cruel, deceitful bastard! I have to give it to you… you played an excellent match. But this is far from over. You have shown your hand, I now know what you've been doing and with whom. You may have won this battle, but there is a war coming Giza, a war from which you nor ANY of your descendants will escape! You hear me! None of you will escape!

Lifeguard: What the hell! Hey, hey... wake up! You can't be up here.

Bellamy and I woke up to the sound of the lifeguard from tower #9.

We must have fallen asleep. Bellamy looked over at me, "did that shit actually happen!" I groaned from soreness as I stood up, "it feels like it did, and these bruises sure do tell a tale". As we walked over to our cars, we were both a bit in shock. I took out my phone and searched for the death of Pearson and the riots, but to my surprise no such information populated. "There's no info about Pearson and him dying, nor about us being all big and godly".

Bellamy: Damn! I mean I'm glad he didn't die... but I was hoping we would officially become superheroes. At least we still tatted tho, so that must mean something. Maybe we can tap into our powers from time to time.

Leslie: Yeah, and we actually did what we had to. That's pretty awesome!

Bellamy: I have I told you that I love your mind? You get so deep with it.

Leslie: You may have mentioned it before.

Bellamy: Uh, Still got that blunt?

Leslie: Oh, you want smoke? Come on, I got you.

As me and Bell both go into my car and closed the doors, we were instantly transported. Bellamy clutched my arm in confusion, "Yo, Croney... where the fuck are we?" As I looked around, I remembered the broken atmosphere of Origen from previous visions. Without giving myself a moment to explain, I slid my right hand over to my left forearm and pinched it. I notice Bellamy did the same, then we looked at each other… "I can feel that shit".

Special thanks...

Firstly, I have to give a shout out to two people that took the time to invest in my authorship.

Firstly, to my friend, my woe, my sis Jenipher "J" Croney for taking the time out to listen as I shared my ideas about Origen with her over the years. I am so grateful for your patience, insight, and honesty. I respect and count on your wisdom as well as editing skills.

Secondly, to my FSU comrade, IT guru and Web Designer Marcelina Nagales, I so appreciate you taking the time to journey with me. We both know that I would have NOT been able to put this digital space together on my own.

May the energy that sustains you, never rest and forever reign!

Ms. Stephanie Croney

www.origencreators.world

www.origencreators@gmail.com

Areas of Concentration

Religious Literature, Afrofuturism, Cultural Anthropology, Afro-descendancy, Magical Realism, Cultural Studies, Digital Humanities, Artistic Expressions, Critical Race Theory and Design Thinking

Stephanie Croney's current research through Florida State University and independently, analyzes the historical foundation of stigmatizing, imaging, and labeling of Afro descendant women and culture alongside Afrofuturism as a representation, tool, genre, authentic expression and mechanism of cultural autonomy and identity. Stephanie utilizes Afrofuturism, Hip Hop Culture, and cultural experience to produce works that highlight and address concerns and evolutionary processes of Afro descendant peoples across space and time.

Independent Works

- Croney. Origen: Beginning. Amazon Kindle Publishing. 2022
  Origen: Beginning is the first installation to the Origen series by Croney. The narrative is based upon dreams, premonitions, and imagination by the author. The story follows Leslie, a 35-year-old single mother of two through a series of spiritual realities as she becomes enlightened about her divine ancestry and prophetic purpose.

References:

"Anh Sang" (Light beam in Vietnamese). https://en.bab.la.vietnamese-english. Accessed: July 25, 2022

"Asteri" (Star in Greek). www.names.org. Accessed: July 25, 2022.

Brandy. 1994. "Brandy: I Wanna Be Down". Keith Crouch.

Chakra Stone Chart. www.7chakrastore.com. Accessed: July 25, 2022.

Collins, Patricia and Sirma Bilge. 2016. Intersectionality. Polity Press. Cambridge, UK.

"Deities of the Yoruba and Fon Religions" World Eras Encyclopedia. Accessed: 10 June 2022. https://www.encyclopedia.com/history/news-wires-white-papers-and-books/dieties-yoruba-and-fon-religions

DMX. 1998. "It's Dark and Hell is Hot: Niggaz Done Started Something". Def Jam; Ruff Ryders

"Elohi" (Earth in Cherokee). www.native-language.org. Accessed: August 10, 2018

Higher Frequencies. 2021. "Meditation, Yoga, Sleep and Healing Solfeggio Frequencies: Releasing Fear (Solfeggio 396 Hz)".

"Inaru" (Woman in Taino). www.native-language.org. Accessed: August 10, 2018.

King, Dr. Martin Luther. 1957. "Loving your Enemies" Sermon Delivered at Dexter Avenue Baptist Church Montgomery, AL. www.okra.standford.edu. Accessed: 6 June 2022

"ofrenda" (Spanish for offering/alter). www.thegracemuseum.org Accessed: July 27, 2022

Rhys, Dani. "Oya, The Goddess of Weather" Symbolsage: Understanding the World Through Symbols and Mythology. www.symbolsgae.com. Accessed July 2, 2021.

Royster, Jacqueline Jones. 2000. Trace of a Stream: Literacy and Social Change Among African American Women. University of Pittsburgh Press. Pittsburgh, PA.

The Temptations. 1971. "Sky's the Limit: Just My Imagination". Gordy G 7105.

"We ride together, we die together…" https://badboys.fandom.com. Accessed: July 27, 2022

Winfrey, Oprah. 2017. The Wisdom of Sunday: Life-Changing Insights from Super Soul Conversations. Flatiron Book. New York, NY.

"You got knocked the f out…" https://www.quotes.net. Accessed: July 27, 2022.

*This text mentions terms, people, places, and things known in our present world as well as imagined and are used to highlight a sense of togetherness and never used to misrepresent anyone, anything, or any time.

Made in the USA
Coppell, TX
25 September 2022

83576986R00118